I0671934

FIND THE FALLEN
Guardians of the Fae Realms: Book 13
JL Madore

Copyright © 2022

All rights reserved. No part of this publication may be reproduced, distributed or transmitted in any form or by any means, without prior written permission.

JL Madore

Cover Design: Gombar Cover Designs

Note: The moral right of the author has been asserted.

This is a work of fiction. Names, characters, places and incidents either are the product of the author's imagination or are used fictitiously, and any resemblance to actual persons, living or dead, business establishments, events, or locales is entirely coincidental.

No part of this publication may be reproduced, stored in a retrieval system or transmitted, in any form or by any means without the prior written permission of the author, nor be otherwise circulated in any form of binding or cover other than that in which it is published and without a similar condition being imposed on the subsequent buyer.

The scanning, uploading, and distribution of this book via the Internet or via any other means without the permission of the author is illegal and punishable by law. Please purchase only authorized electronic editions, and do not participate in or encourage electronic piracy of copyrighted materials.

Your support of the author's rights is appreciated.

Find The Fallen : Guardians of the Fae Realms

JL Madore -- 1st ed.

ISBN: 978-1-998372-70-6

BEFORE YOU START!
Find the Fallen is book one in Lark's harem and book 13 in The Guardians of the Fae Realms series.
If you missed the first three harems, and want the intro to how we got here, you can grab the books below and start at book 1 of the entire series.
Guardians of the Phoenix.
Darkness Calls
Book 9 – Honor Restored
Book 10 – Honor Guards
Book 11 – Honor Bound
Book 12 – Honor Empowered

If you don't want to, that's fine too. The story stands alone, there might just be characters you don't know.
To that end:
Calli is the phoenix, and her guardians are Kotah (Wolf), Jaxx (Jaguar), Hawk (Hawk...obvi), and Brant (Bear)

Keyla came next with Creed (Mind Guardian Fae), Dillan/Doc (Bear) and Rhylan (Dragon)

Honor Thornebane is King Creed's sister and in charge of quadrant security. Her mates are Lukas (mage), Shadow (Elf Oracle), Tundra and Dune (Amberloq warriors)

CHAPTER ONE

Lark

Two years ago, no one knew our homes would be destroyed, our warriors exterminated, and our people slaughtered. When the forces came, the armies weren't powerful, they were filthy, traitorous goblin thugs with the Blood Witch behind them and a corrupt bitch behind her, hell-bent on stealing the crown.

The Usurper Queen.

For two years that black-souled bitch terrorized the quadrant, allowing the greedy and corrupt to get rich while the citizens of Dornte suffered.

And then, the Phoenix was born.

Calliope Tanis, now known as Calli, was an ordinary street rat human who wrapped her car around a power pole and died.

That's when the fae universe stepped in and changed the course of everything that followed.

Calli's guardians were activated, they re-established the portal gate between the Human Realm and the Fae Realm of

StoneHaven, and the Usurper Queen moved to expand her queendom.

King Creed laid eyes on a young wolf wildling, fell in love, and found the strength to reclaim his throne.

His sister, Honor, was rescued from her imprisonment in a lead vault and she reclaimed her place safeguarding the Crown of Dornte.

And then she and her mates, in turn, rescued me.

It boggles the mind when you think about it. If one of those things hadn't happened... If Calli hadn't figured out how to reunite the realms...

If King Creed hadn't been able to take down the Usurper and the Blood Witch...

If Honor hadn't sent her mates out to find survivors... maybe I, and the people I protected for two years, might still be imprisoned.

It's mind boggling.

The Elbirfae elders believe it's the will of the fae universe. I have no opinion on that either way. All I know is that after two years of living under the whip and blade of goblins, we're free and I don't know what to do with all the baggage I'm carrying.

I pump my wings and close my eyes, dropping toward the trees until I feel the pocket of air cool above the foliage. On instinct alone, I level out and skim the top of the canopy. The beauty of the Forest and Jungle Biome is making a comeback.

The villages in the trees are being rebuilt, and the rubble of the homes of our past are being swallowed by the dense regrowth. But even as more and more of the evidence of violence disappears, and the people I protected begin to rebuild their lives, my anger and isolation never fade.

I thrust forward, my wings pumping hard, the muscles in my back aching from the hours of torment I've been putting them through. I close my eyes again, feel the wind hit my face, and pull my hair with the speed of my flight.

No matter how fast I fly or how hard I push, I can't outrun the emotions churning inside me. I try to act civilized, but maybe I lost more than my freedom in those two years.

Flipping in mid-air to face the moons of Dornte, I give voice to my fury and scream. Long and loud, my cry fills the sky until my vocal cords ache. When I think I've scared enough birds from the treetops, I fall silent and focus on breathing.

They say this will pass.

I've spoken to a dozen of my people who spend time with the royal counselor, Shadow. He encourages them to feel their emotions, acknowledge what happened, and then leave it in the past.

I've never gone to speak to the blind Oracle myself. I can't. I'm the one who holds everyone else together. If they knew I was as much of a mess as I am, they'd lose confidence in my leadership.

And if I spill my innermost terrors to Shadow, sure as shit Princess Honor will hear about it. I have no doubt patient confidentiality doesn't apply to pillow talk. Shadow could share my instability with his mates and then I'd be screwed.

Arriving at Amberloq Hall, the security compound found on the grounds of Thornebane Castle, I land and draw a deep breath. The incursion team for tonight's mission is relatively small—a security squad from the Human Realm, Princess Honor, her human mate, Lukas, and Tundra and Dune, two of her other mates, my Amberloq counterparts for the Snowy Peaks and Desert Biomes.

I'm both anticipating and anxious about tonight's mission. They are all trained soldiers—I'm a survivor. Dune and Tundra are Amberloq warriors—I'm not.

I'm not sure if everyone here knows I got the honorary position to lead my biome because I was the only Forested Jungle alpha left standing... but *I* know.

And so do the Princess and her mates.

"Lark, good, you're here," Princess Honor says, striding over to join me. The female is tall and confident, with the poise of a royal and the grace of a trained fae warrior. "We're ready to hit the skies. Are you good to go?"

"Yes, Princess."

Honor turns to face her soldiers, her long, silver braid gliding through the night air like a whip. "Mac, is your squad ready to take flight?"

Her attention is directed toward Connor MacDougall, a well-built and chiseled soldier with a mop of shoulder-length, russet red curls. I don't know the man well, but he was part of the infiltration team that rescued us, and he helped get my people settled in our new home.

He seems like a decent soldier—or as decent as a human soldier can be.

"Aye, Princess. Ready and waitin' on yer orders," he says, flashing her a smile.

She releases her ebony and turquoise wings and fans them out behind her. Then she nods to Lukas. "Fire up your bird, magic man. It's go time."

Lukas winks and opens the door to the helicopter. Those without wings will use the air machine to fly to the foothills in the Dornte Fringe. "See you there, beautiful. Comms check."

She touches the small transmitter in her ear and gives him a thumbs up. "Comms are up."

Tundra, the Amberloq General for the Snowy Peaks, taps his earpiece and nods. "Check."

And then Dune, the Amberloq General for the Desert biome, nods as well. "Check."

Their gazes swing as one toward me and I tap the communication device in my ear. "Comms are up."

With that, the rotors of the sleek, mechanical bird start to spin faster, and we all take to the air.

~

As we close the distance to our meeting point, Honor opens the comms channel and goes over the night's objective. "Our contact is a local fire fairy named Remi. She tends bar at a place called the Gauntlet and has been helpful to the extreme. She's to be considered a valued asset. I assured her no matter what happens, nothing will blow back on her."

"And she'll be leadin' us inta the foothills personally, lass?" Connor asks.

"Does that matter?"

"Och, no, but it does make me trust her intel a little more. If she were settin' us up fer an ambush, she wouldna want to be sittin' in the truck next to us when it happens."

"Good point, and yes, she's coming with us."

"That's good then," he says.

"Remi has arranged for a small caravan of trucks with off-road capability to get us to the compound. From what my aunt said in the instructions she left me, her super soldier program is, or at least was, being run by a scientist named Andras Brass and his team."

"Do we know anything about Brass?" I ask.

"Not much. He was born and raised in Travon, excelled as a student, and went to further his education at the StoneHaven Institute of Science and Innovation where he was asked to join the faculty."

"SISI? Holy shit," Dune says, flying close on my right. "Brass has gray matter."

"I think that's evident from him developing a super soldier program," Tundra says.

Dune laughs. "No need to be frosty, Ice Man."

I watch Dune, Tundra, and Princess Honor as the three of them fly. They seem genuinely happy. And when she's with Lukas and Shadow, the five of them seem happy as well.

5

I don't get it.

I've never enjoyed dating and being accountable to another person, let alone four other people. Too many cooks in the kitchen, if you ask me.

Then again, nobody asked me.

The tactical watch on my wrist vibrates and I bring it around to read the incoming message. It's a proximity warning. We're almost at the coordinates of the meeting point.

Honor checks her watch as well and begins to drop altitude. "Time to get this party started, boys and girls. Meet you on the ground."

I draw a deep breath and follow. Making my mark and proving to Honor and her mates that I'm the right person to lead the Forested Jungle Biome is imperative. I won't let them take from me the respect and leadership I earned over the past two years.

I can learn to be a team player.

I can learn to be a skilled warrior.

For the good of the citizens of Dornte, and the decimated Amberloq army, I will rise to any challenge and rebuild the image of my biome.

As the first-ever female Biome General, I can show the quadrant how to grab the reins of life and be the change they want to see.

Honor and her two Amberloq lovers land beside three gray, black, and beige all-terrain trucks. Dune begins to examine them the moment his massive brown falcon's wings fold behind him.

Lukas cuts the power on the rotor blades of the helicopter and their bird stops screeching. Damn that thing is noisy.

If you ask me, that's unnecessary noise pollution.

Except, once again, no one asked me.

Mac

Lukas touches the bird down in the foothills of the Dornte Fringe and I check in with my squadron. "Ready and steady, lads and lasses?"

"Right and tight," Josie says back, her hand on the handle of the door.

"All clear," Lukas says, the hum of the rotors slowing. "Keep your heads down."

"Thanks fer the lift, Squad Leader."

"My pleasure, Mac. Are you ready to show the quadrant what Alpha Squadron is made of?"

"Ready, sir. Just give us enough rein to do our thing and we'll make ye proud."

Lukas nods. "You always do, my friend."

As he heads over to confer with his mates, I raise my hand to quiet my team. "Tazz and Dwa, I want a vehicle sweep. No one steps foot into any of those vehicles until ye clear them. Drix and Martin, give me a three-sixty. I don't want any surprises. Blue, yer on sniper watch. The rest of ye grab our gear and transfer vehicles. Quick and quiet, people."

As Alpha Squad kicks into gear, I take a moment to scan the horizon. It's good to be back in Dornte.

There's something about the magic of this place that feeds my cells.

That's not hyperbole.

There is actual magic in the air here that isn't present back home. It calls to the predator prowling inside my veins. It emboldens the furry beast and I'm not going to pretend I don't like it.

It's like having a constant battle hard-on ready to put to good use. How could that be bad?

"Are you good, Mac?" Honor offers me a curious smile.

"Aye, Princess. Never better."

She takes a step into my personal space, facing the landscape behind me. Leaning close, her lips whisper just above my shoulder. "Keep an eye on Lark, will you? For all she's been through, she's not a soldier and is too damned headstrong to admit it."

"I can do that, Princess."

She touches my wrist, and the contact sends another surge of magic through my system. "Thanks, Mac. I appreciate all you do for us."

I clear my throat and try not to look too closely at my body's reaction. "Not a problem, Princess."

Stepping away, I make busy work of checking my guns and overseeing my squad. It won't do to have her mates smelling my current state of arousal near their female.

Lukas would understand. He knows better about the predator I share space with, but still, I value him both as a friend and a commanding officer.

Besides, it's not Honor that has me cock-hard and randy. It's this blessed quadrant. Something about Dornte is like an aphrodisiac, a feel-good party drug ramping me up for a wild night.

When everyone is busy prepping for the mission, I step into the shelter of the vehicles to assess the female in question.

Lark of the Forested Jungle Biome.

She's tall and physically fit, as most Elbirfae are. She's also stunningly beautiful. Her wings and hair are raven black and seem to absorb the daylight around her to shroud her in shadow.

If she had the inclination, she could be a damned good assassin with a natural trait like that.

Her wings aren't the massive, eight-foot-long affair like the males of her species. Where Tundra and Dune have wings cresting above the back of their heads and taper to fall at the back of their leather boots, Lark's wings stop just beneath the rounds of her very fine ass.

As if she can feel the heat of my gaze, she turns, picks me out of the organized chaos of deployment, and glares.

And then there are her eyes...

Those windows into her soul are as brilliant green as the lushest leaves in the forest with a hint of dark shadows edging in when the wind blows her way. But, beyond the vibrancy, there's a sadness that calls to my beast. The woman's been knocked down and come back swinging.

The problem is, she's safe now and still swinging.

"Vehicles clear, sir," Jazz says, breaking the focus of the stare down. "Aye. Thanks, soldier. Load 'em up then and let's rock and roll."

Once the vehicles are deemed safe, the gear is loaded, and the squad takes their positions. Some slide into the seats and some will ride on the outside, like me. I step onto the running board of the rear truck, grip the roof rack, and knock on the steel roof to signal our departure.

The truck kicks off with a jolt and then the caravan is in motion. Two of my men are wildlings and take to the skies with the Elbirfae and the princess.

The rest of us settle in for the ride.

Lark

The terrain of the Dornte Fringe is rough and uninviting. For those riding in the conveyances, I'm sure their teeth and bones are rattling under the jostle of the axel-eating pits and crevices the trucks are navigating.

The ride is smooth sailing in the skies.

I laugh to myself even though it's not charitable. Sucks to be you, humans.

Maybe they'll take the hint from the land's welcome and realize they don't belong here.

"Harsh," Dune says, glancing over at me. "You better not let Honor or the others hear you say anything like that, or you'll be shown the door PDQ."

"PDQ?"

"Pretty damned quick."

I gauge the distance between us and Tundra and the Princess on one side of us and the two squad soldiers that have transformed into a golden eagle and the falcon on the other side.

Thankfully only Dune was within earshot.

"I didn't realize nor intend to speak aloud. My comment was inappropriate but wasn't meant for outside ears."

Dune looks over at me and chuckles. "The comment isn't nearly as worrying as the fact that you seem to believe that bullshit."

I roll my eyes. "Forget I said anything."

"Nope. Sorry. Honor and Creed are working their asses off to unite the quadrant and that includes the *entire* quadrant. They're firm about prejudices having no place in their governing structure. If you've got a problem with humans coming through the portal gate, you need to either get over it or remove yourself from a leadership position."

Now it's my turn to laugh. "Are you serious? You, of all people, can say that to me with a straight face?"

Dune's gaze narrows and the hair at the nape of my neck stands on end. "What do you mean by that?"

"Just that I've heard the rumors about you and the struggles you had accepting the new order."

Dune's smile grows icy. "Choose your next words wisely, female, because your future as a biome representative depends on it."

Slecking hell.

How did I step in it so badly, so quickly?

"My apologies. I shouldn't have said anything. I didn't mean to offend."

"That might be true, but you did. And for your information, Alpha Squad was integral in breaking you out of that gods forsaken goblin prison. They also saved my life when we destroyed the weapons bunker. They're also a highly-skilled team made up of really great people."

"Humans," I say, clarifying. "Not people. Or at least not *our* people."

"Our people? They've got humans, wildlings, a couple of them have Elven blood, I think one of them is part gnome. What does that have to do with it? Are you one of those idiots who believes we should've kept the two realms separate?"

"A gate radical? No." I draw a deep breath looking for any way to end this conversation. "I think it's amazing that the bridge between realms is reinstated. There were fae citizens over there who had family here and desperately missed them. There were fae people who had to hide themselves in the Human Realm who can now live here and be free to fly their fae flag with pride. I think that's amazing."

"But just not the humans?"

I shrug. "Honestly, I figure they have their realm, and we have ours. No need to muddy those waters."

"You realize one of my mates is human, right? Are you saying Lukas, a man who literally saved your ass from goblin torture has no right to be here?"

I wave away the fury building in the air between us. "Seriously, forget I said anything. I'm just anxious about the mission and let my mind get carried away. Please don't say anything. My mind was just spinning up bullshit and my mouth didn't have the sense to keep it to myself."

Dune pegs me with a stern look. "I've certainly been known to spout shit myself. So, for now, I'll drop it. But if I hear or see anything that leads me to believe this wasn't just nerves, you can bet your silky black feathers I'll catch my mates up on your world views and we'll show you to the door."

I meet his gaze with all the seriousness I have within me. "Understood, General. That won't be necessary. You have my word."

My tactical watch vibrates, and I tilt it to read the incoming message.

Dune does the same. "Looks like we're here."

With a graceful tilt of his muscled wings, the wind catches his feathers, and he plummets for the rocky ground below.

Shit. Shit. Shit.

And here I thought this might not go well.

CHAPTER TWO

Lark

While Honor and Lukas take last minute direction from the fire fairy bartender, I watch the humans unload their gear and get ready for battle.

This compound was originally established by Honor's aunt and predecessor, Valorous. It's been two years since she was murdered, and no one knew to come check the progress of her super soldier program.

Maybe Valorous' death ended the experiments.

Maybe the Usurper Queen caught wind of the objectives when she seized the throne and intervened.

Maybe all is well, and they continued on without an overseer.

No one has any answers and therefore we don't know what to expect.

"Yer to stick close to me in there, lass," Connor Mac says in his thick brogue.

The sound of him right behind me is both startling and infuriating. As a warrior, I should be aware of people approaching at all times.

I swear, the man treads as lightly as a cat.

"With not knowin' what's what, yer Guardian of the Crown asked that I keep ye close."

I turn and meet his gaze. "I assure you, that's not necessary, soldier."

"Whether it is or it isn't is of no matter. An order from a superior is just that—an order. Come now, let's get ye fitted up with some weapons. We can't have ye facin' genetically modified super soldiers with only a wee poker, now, can we?"

I press a hand to the dagger sheathed against my thigh. "I'm fine. I didn't ask for your help, nor do I need it."

Amusement dances in his hazel eyes. "Be that as it may, ye got it. Now come along. Compounds to raid, battles to win, and all that."

I make no move to follow. "I appreciate the concern, but I'll be fine. I can take care of myself."

He steps forward and squares off with me. All traces of amusement drain from his expression, and I'm left with a cold, hard glare. "Let me make this plain fer ye, lass, because I think somethin' got lost in translation. Everyone else on this mission is a trained soldier. *They* can take care of themselves. Yer a liability and are too stubborn or too arrogant to realize it."

"Excuse me? You don't know—"

He strikes forward faster than should be possible. His hand clasps my throat as he sweeps my ankle and drops me to the dirt. He follows the momentum, pinning me on the ground with a knee to my chest and my body held tightly in his grip.

He gives me a moment to let that sink in.

He didn't even try.

"—I *do* know, and I'm not finished yet, so shut yer gob until I am."

My wings flex, fighting to flare behind me to push me from the ground.

I shove at him... and get nowhere.

He leans forward and the air around us rumbles with a predatory growl.

My heart races as I search the wildness in his gaze. Being pinned beneath him both infuriates and intrigues me. There is an animalistic quality to him I haven't seen before. "What are you?"

His anger melts into a heated smile. "I'm a predator and yer prey. So ye better not look at me like that, little bird, or ye'll be gettin' much more than ye meant to from me."

My instincts roar with the need to grab hold of him and prove that I can take anything he can give. And with his erection pressed hard against my thigh, I have a good idea of what that would be.

He draws a deep breath and lets off a quiet purr.

"Och, I wish we had the time to take care of yer wanton, little bird, but alas, it'll have to wait."

I laugh. "You're so slecking arrogant."

He snaps his teeth together and leans close, his deep red hair falling forward to brush the sides of my cheeks. "Aye, but I admit it. Ye see, that's the difference between us, love. I acknowledge my strengths *and* my weaknesses. That way, I'm not surprised if someone's able to exploit them."

I fight against his hold once again and still get nowhere. How is he so slecking strong?

After a moment, I stop fighting him and he eases back to give me space. "Ye've got fight. I admire that. Bein' a scrapper and survivin' a bad situation is commendable. I'll not take that away from ye, lass."

"You couldn't if you tried."

"Right, but ye rose to be the top fighter in a controlled and contained situation. Ye kept yer charges safe and most of ye made it out. This isn't that."

I'm sure we're attracting unwanted attention, but I refuse to give him the satisfaction of dropping my gaze. He might be a predator, but I'm not submissive.

"This is an infiltration and possible extraction, ye see. Yer not trained fer it and if ye feck it up, or things go sideways and ye zig when ye shoulda zagged, yer endangerin' *my* people. I'll not have that."

"Then go home and take your people and leave Dornte problems to the people of Dornte."

He straightens and laughs. "Is that what this is? Yer feelin' territorial, are ye? Weel, now, let me set ye straight on that. Yer quadrant currently has the military might of yer princess, her three Amberloq mates and the King's dragon mate. The royal couple can defend themselves in a pinch, but it'll not do yer quadrant any good to have them battlin' out on the lines."

"What's your point?"

"My point is that the Dornte military is in shambles and the folks in power recognize it. They called in me and mine because we're better trained, better armed, and better prepared to take on the dangers of yer realm. If ye don't like it, then launch yerself into the skies and fly away home, little bird, because yer not welcome here if ye don't tone down yer attitude and start towin' the fuckin' line."

"How dare you?"

"He's right," Honor says, drawn to the scene. "Let her up, Mac."

The male flashes me a grin and springs to his feet, pulling me to mine in a move so strong and graceful it makes my head spin.

Honor waits for me to brush off my butt and shake out my wings before she continues. "Street fighting and surviving isn't the same as Amberloq training, even if retired Amberloq warriors were there to guide you. I asked Mac to keep you close for your safety. If you're going to make this harder than it needs to be on Alpha Squad, maybe you sitting this one out isn't such a bad idea."

I stiffen and clench my fingers into fists. "I assure you, that won't be necessary, Princess."

Her gaze is narrowed on mine, and I know she's assessing my sincerity.

"While I'm both disheartened and offended to be assigned a babysitter, if that is your final word on the matter, I accept it."

Honor shakes her head. "It's not babysitting, Lark. You have yet to realize that you don't know what you don't know. Trust Mac. Listen to his commands and observe his team in action. I'm not saying you don't have skills—you do—they just aren't honed yet. You being disruptive ripples throughout the entire team and I won't allow that."

I swallow the bile burning at the back of my throat. "I understand, Princess. Consider me in line."

She gives me a nod and moves off to finish preparations.

I meet Connor's gaze with all the fury I can offer him. "Now that you've humiliated me and made me look bad in front of the Princess, why don't you go ahead and get me that gun. I'm ready to use it."

Mac

She's got fight, I'll give her that. After Honor has her say, the little black bird submits. She's like a wild stallion being forced to take a saddle. She's not going to accept it without kicking up a good deal of dust.

And while I find it alluring as a man, I don't think much of it as a commander. Still, the problems that creates won't be solved just now.

"Brody, what can ye tell me?"

My second in command jogs over and pulls his tablet from the wide pocket in the thigh of his fatigues. "We got geothermal from the soil on the far side of the driveway, but no sign of movement inside."

"How fresh are the heat signatures in the soil?"

"I'd guess twenty-minutes max."

"Are Drix and Blue in the air?"

"Yeah. I gave them a five-mile leash to see if they could catch up to the vehicle that bugged out. If they don't find anything by then, their orders are to circle back and join the infiltration in progress."

"What do we know about the building itself?"

He pulls up the schematics.

One of the nicest things about working for Hawk Barron and the Fae Concealment Office is the toys. If there's bleeding edge technology on the market in either realm, we've got it first.

Brody taps the screen of his tablet and a three-dimensional view of the building lights up in white architectural lines on a black screen.

I reach over, assessing the entrances and possible pinch points we need to be wary of. Tapping the screen, I drag the building around and tilt it to see the lower stories from a better angle. "What the hell is happenin' here?"

"I think that's the real target, Mac. After looking at this, I'm betting the building above ground will be a cover and the real magic happened in the nine bunker levels below."

I tap the comm and open a line. After relaying that information, I voice my only concern. "Alpha Squad will need ta check the lower levels before I sign off on the Princess headin' down. If there's been a switch in allegiance over the past two years, the whole place could be booby-trapped to keep pryin' eyes out."

"Copy that, Alpha-1," Lukas says. "We'll stay topside while you do your thing."

I nod to Brody and speak off comms. "I want infra readers, explosive sniffers, and signal jammers down there with us."

"Got them."

"Aye, then we're good to go." Opening the channel once more, I draw my sidearm and take the lead. "Alpha Squadron on the move."

~

Lark

I stay behind with Honor and the others as Alpha Squad breaches. Lukas has their body cams hooked into our feed and I follow them on the screen of my watch. Divided into three teams, they enter the building from the front, back, and side. They move as one and despite my run-in with their team leader, I respect what they do and how they do it.

So why do I fight so hard?

I'm not even sure. There's something about people pushing at me that makes me push back. Maybe it's the years in the goblin's camp being toyed with for their amusement, or maybe it's ingrained in my genetics somehow.

I've never been one to lose ground to anyone... even before the raids and our capture.

"Sector two, clear," someone says into my ear.

"Sector three, clear," another soldier says.

"Sector one, clear," Mac says. "The main building is cleared to enter, Princess."

There's no missing the sweetness in his voice as he says her title. I don't get it. Why do all these powerful, dominant men circle her and yet get sweet and protective of her?

Is it a princess thing? Does being a royal really turn heads? Who cares? She's just an ordinary woman who happened to be born to the leader of a quadrant.

"Any sign of super soldiers, Mac?" Honor asks.

"Nothin' yet, Princess, but there are still sections we haven't gained access to. This ain't over yet. Alpha Squad movin' to secure the lower levels."

"Stay sharp everyone. Be safe."

We wait and watch a while longer until Alpha Squad gains access to the lower levels and starts to systematically search the underground floors.

Lukas watches his men with pride, tracking their movements until the coverage goes spotty. When the sound and video start flickering in and out, he checks with us. "Everyone ready to move out?"

We all nod.

"Dune, you're in the air until Drix and Blue return. One of you three will remain as our eyes in the sky until you're relieved."

"Understood."

"Heads on a swivel, people."

I'm not exactly comfortable using a gun as my weapon. I've handled blasters when I've had to, but for the most part, I'm more of a dagger in the shadows fighter or straight on hand-to-hand.

Being Elbirfae helps with both of those.

With my ebony wings, I can fight and blend into shadows. My height gives me an edge over most fairy species. And my ability to fly is an asset which, while not rare in the fae realm, is still uncommon enough that I can use it to my advantage.

But, if the Princess wants me to play nice with her pet human and her pet human wants me to carry a gun, I'll carry the gun.

Getting inside didn't offer Alpha Squad much of a challenge and after fifteen minutes of them searching the lower levels, it's apparent why.

"Whoever was here took the goods and hit the ground

runnin'," Mac says, when he returns to ground level to update us. "They left in a hurry, but they are definitely gone."

"Do you think they'll come back?" I ask.

"Doubtful. At least... not until they think we've cleared out, I'm sure."

"Who tipped them off we were coming, Mac?"

"Can't say as of yet, but my guess is either a local getting paid to notify them if anyone comes snoopin' or perimeter surveillance we missed."

Lukas waves that away. "I highly doubt that. Send Drix or Blue over our approach route and see where we would've raised any eyebrows. If it was a tip, maybe they can tell us who paid them."

"Maybe we can trace a currency account and get a line on who's behind things now," Tundra says.

"Good idea, T."

Mac taps his earpiece. "Brody, have Drix and Blue checked in?"

"Not yet, sir."

"Weel, let me know when they do."

"You got it. And boss? You may want to bring the Princess to subfloor four. Josie found a console with an interface intact. She's hotwiring it now to see if we can get anything off it. Also, there's a security door down here with writing on it we can't read."

Mac checks with Lukas and the princess and then nods. "On our way."

CHAPTER THREE

Lark

$\mathcal{M}$ ac sends one of his men out to keep watch for his two other soldiers and Dune rejoins our group. When our Amberloq squad is reassembled, we head to the lower levels.

The elevators in the building are massive. Normally, because of the height of Elbirfae and the space needed to incorporate the wings of males, when my people go anywhere in a group, elevators make things difficult.

The elevator in this building could take one of the all-terrain vehicles into the lower levels and we'd still have space to spread our wings.

"Roomy," Dune says, echoing my thoughts. To further the point, he waves his elbows and flares his wings in the empty space.

"It's kind of like this place was designed by the Amberloq to accommodate the size of Elbirfae warriors," Honor says, grinning at him.

He laughs. "I guess that makes sense."

The small chime rings off, announcing our arrival at the fourth floor below ground. After a gentle bump, the doors slide open.

Outside the metal doors of the elevators, a long room is set up as an administration area with two long desks on the right and left and a pathway down the center that leads to a set of secured double doors.

A female warrior from Alpha Squad is set up at one of the desks working on establishing a connection with a data terminal that seems to have been recently assaulted by a very large...

"Sledgehammer." Dune picks up the weapon of technological destruction. "What did that data terminal ever do to them?"

Lukas chuckles. "It's hard to miss with something like that. Maybe they just wanted to be sure."

"Well, if we're still in business, they must've missed anyway."

The woman in uniform raises her attention and shakes her head. "They didn't so much miss as hit the wrong things."

"Can ye piece it back together, Josie?" Mac asks.

"Yep, I think so. Give me two more minutes and we'll be in business."

"What about the surveillance feeds?" Mac asks, pointing to the cameras mounted over the elevators and by the doors.

"We haven't found a control room yet. It might be hidden down here, or the surveillance might all be sent to a remote location and stored on a cloud."

"Aye, weel, do yer best, lass. I have no doubt ye'll figure it out." The affection in Mac's voice returns. So, it's not just the Princess he fancies, it's the female soldier on his squad too.

I step into the background and watch him interact with the people around him. He's in charge, and yet he's friendly and flirtatious. Still, the moment he encounters a threat, he's as lethal as any warrior I've ever seen. A predator, he said.

I don't doubt that.

After feeling his growl vibrate in my chest, I know there's a beast within him somewhere.

"Princess, when ye have a moment." The blond soldier who leans out from the secured doors and calls her attention is the same male who's always orbiting around Mac. I think his name is Brody and he's Mac's second in command.

"Give me two, Brody," she says, lifting her gaze.

"Yes, Princess."

"What do you need, my man?" Lukas asks.

"Everything in here is written in a fae language we don't understand. I'd like to finish a preliminary sweep in case there is anything time sensitive."

Lukas looks to Tundra, Dune, and me. "Maybe you three can help him out?"

"Of course," Tundra says.

I follow my two counterparts through the secure doors and into the next section of the building.

"Now we're getting somewhere," Dune says, grinning as he takes in the series of labs stretching out before us. "Looks like this is where the magic happened."

Tundra grunts. "Magic? It's more like a scientific nightmare if you ask me."

Me too, though I'm careful not to voice my opinion on that. I've learned my lesson.

Dune steps into the room on the left and takes a look around. "This appears to be a control center of some sort. I bet these view screens look in on another section of the floor."

Tundra looks at me and then tilts his head. "Let's see if we can help Brody access the linguistic information he needs to complete his sweep."

I fall in behind Tundra's broad, white wings and take in the space. It's hard to believe a woman as strong and tactical as Valorous Thornebane could've thought this was a good idea.

"In here," Brody says, holding the door open while we pass

him to enter. "We've been learning the basics of the languages of the realms, but none of us has any idea what this says."

"That's because it's not an official language of the realm," Tundra says. "It's an Amberloq dialect that only warriors would understand or be able to read."

"Perfect, then you know what it says."

Tundra nods. "I do."

While the two of them start working on unlocking the mysteries of these rooms, I explore.

One thing that my mind keeps kicking up to the surface is the amount of money an operation like this would cost.

"It makes you wonder if she spent all this money on training and supporting her regular Amberloq forces if she would've needed super soldiers."

"Aye, that's a fair point," Mac says. "I'd take one of my men over a genetically engineered soldier programmed to fight any day of the week."

Wonders never cease—we agree on something.

Not that I'd admit that to him.

"So, the ones that evacuated? Do you think that was the scientists, the soldiers, or both?"

"Too early to tell, lass. Hopefully, when my boys get back, they'll be able to tell us more."

I move to look at another set of doors, running my fingers over the writing on the placard on the wall. The fact that I can't read it is yet another reminder that I'm not truly an Amberloq warrior.

The metallic click in front of me snaps my attention to the door. It hisses and slides open, granting me entry into a sterile antechamber.

"Well done, boys," I call over my shoulder.

I move forward, and Mac protests. "Hold. Let me get in there first, lass."

As if.

"It's a little, empty space. No hostiles. No threat. No need for you to flex your military muscles."

I continue forward, my gaze locked on the console positioned in the center of the room. There's a stack of papers scattered over the top of the metal surface.

Mac follows quickly and scowls at me as he secures the room. "Ye need to listen a bit better, lass. We're still in an unknown state here."

"I think you're forgetting I'm an Amberloq General. I don't need your protection or your permission."

He arches a brow. "I think yer fergettin' yer boss told ye ta start listenin' or shove off."

I ignore his rant and focus on the papers in front of me. *Finally, something I can dig into.*

The two of us sidle up to the console, him on the opposite side facing me. He swings some of the papers toward himself to read and I pretend he's not here.

There are a bunch of graphs, scientific findings that make no sense to me, and observations jotted down in an illegible shorthand that probably acted as someone's private code.

"Hey, you got the door open," Brody says, stepping in to join us. "How'd you manage that?"

I glance up from the papers and shrug. "Not us. I figured Tundra or Dune did something in the rooms they're in."

He looks confused. "I don't think so. They just told me they've gotten nowhere."

"Maybe the lass triggered a release," Mac says. "She was standin' outside the door and passed her hand over the panel on the side there."

Brody turns back the way we came and steps out to examine the area Mac indicated. The moment he raises his hand to touch it, the door slams shut.

"Weel, now. I'm not fond of that. What did ye do to offend

her, kid?" he shouts, so his words carry to the other side of the sealed door.

"I'm not sure," Brody's voice comes back muffled. "Maybe I should've bought her dinner before I got touchy feely."

"Apparently. All right. How about ye make it up to her and get that door back open?"

"On it."

I grip the edge of the table, my body frozen. Mac is searching the inside seam of the closed door, so he doesn't seem to notice my momentary panic.

Deep and slow breaths. *I'm fine. No one here will hurt me.* I inhale through my nose drawing air deep into my burning lungs and then exhale out my mouth.

Maybe Mac hears the change in my breathing or maybe his predator senses the weakness of its prey, but he turns around and fixes his gaze on me. "Are ye all right, lass?"

"I'm not a fan of being closed in."

"All right. How bad is it?"

"I... uh, take this from me." I hand him the gun he forced me to carry, and his eyes grow wide. "Better safe than sorry. We haven't gotten along the best today and I tend to get a little defensive and aggressive when I'm trapped."

"Only when yer trapped?"

I try to laugh at his attempt at humor but my hearing is starting to warble and my vision is fritzing in and out. *I'm fine. No one here will hurt me.*

Deep breath in.

Slow exhale out.

"I'm right here with ye, lass. If ye need someone to anchor ye, I'm here. If ye need me just to talk ye through it, I can do that too."

"I'm not weak," I snap. "I'm not a victim."

"Och, I never thought ye were. But ye are scared. I can smell

27

your panic and yer anger, and it sets my beast on edge. Just tell me what to do."

"Get the door open."

There's a deep rumble of male laughter. "That's a given. What else can I do?"

"You're doing it. Just talk to me." I swallow but the action does nothing to moisten my dry mouth.

"Here, take a wee nip of this to settle yer nerves." Mac slides in beside me and unscrews the cap of a small silver flask. "It's strong, so go—"

I grip the smooth container against my lips and tip my head back. The liquid burns its way to the back of my tongue, down my throat, and all the way to my stomach.

Strong is an understatement.

Mac

The lass upends my flask and practically guzzles my best eighty-year-old Scotch whisky. If I wasn't so taken by surprise, I might tell her it's close to three hundred dollars a bottle and is meant to be sipped and savored, but she seems in no mood fer a lesson at present.

When she lowers the flask, she coughs a little but handles the situation better than most men I've shared spirits with.

"Any better, lass?"

She hands me back my flask and returns her hand to grip the edge of the center console. Both hands are braced and clutched around the edge and both hands are white knuckled. With the way she's staring daggers at the far wall, I'm certain whatever she's seein' isn't in the here and now.

"It's all right, lass. Yer safe. Yer people are safe. No one can hurt ye any longer."

She swallows and dips her gaze still locked on the opposite wall. I have half a mind to step around the console to stand before her, but if she's focusing on something I don't see that's anchoring her to the moment, I don't want to interrupt that.

"Yer comin' back now. I see it."

She continues the deep breathing and after a long moment, the tension in her frame starts to ease. "I'm not weak," she repeats, her voice devoid of emotion.

"I never thought it fer a second."

She blinks for the first time in ages and pegs me with a hostile glare. "You don't know... they don't know what we went through... what I went through to keep my people safe and alive."

I force myself not to react. "No, lass, I don't. Sometimes leaders end up carryin' more than their share. I do understand what that's like. I'll not pretend to know yer pain though. That's yers and yers alone."

She blinks, her bright green eyes glassy. "I need out of here, Connor. Please get me out of here."

Her calling me by my first name does something to my insides. I've always respected her fight, so if she's asking for help on this, I know it's bad. "Brody? Any progress, lad?"

"Still working on it."

So, no.

"Don't let that get to ye, lass. It won't be long and if nothin' else, ye got good company." Standing beside her, I reach over to her wrists, grip them, and tug her to turn and face me. "There ye are. Why don't ye glare at me fer a bit and get yer mind off the room around us. I'm nice to look at, aren't I?"

The corner of her mouth quirks up a little and she draws a deep breath. "I'm sure you're well aware you are."

"Aye, but it never hurts a man's ego to hear it."

She chuckles. "I barely even tolerate you."

"That may be true, but that doesn't stop me from drinkin' ye in and thinkin' yer lovely."

"You don't have to charm me. It's not like my destiny led me through all the bullshit of the past two years to leave me to die in an ante chamber. I know we'll get out of here."

"Do ye believe in destiny?"

"To some extent. I believe we control our actions and the cause-and-effect trajectory of our lives but every now and then the fae universe intervenes and throws a detour at us."

"True enough. Many good friends of mine have been sent spinnin' on one of those fae universe detours recently."

She glances down to where I've got a hold of her wrist bracers and I ease up on my grip.

"I may not know everything about everything," she says, "but I know the fae universe is toying with me. Here I am, a survivor of a two-year ordeal, the first Amberloq female in history, and yet, there's more coming for me—I feel it."

I think about the way my cells have been buzzing with fae energy all day and nod. "Aye. I know what that feels like—"

A noise on the other side of the far wall has both of us shifting our attention. I reclaim my weapon from my holster and Lark grabs the one she surrendered.

Both of us lift our weapons and lock our positions.

Guns raised and poised, the two of us freeze.

I tap my earpiece. "This is Alpha-1, we've got movement behind the far wall of the antechamber. Any idea what's on the schematics there?"

"If we go by the plans, nothing," Josie responds.

Lark arches an ebony brow beside me. "We both know that was not nothing."

"Aye we do."

CHAPTER FOUR

Lark

$\mathcal{M}$ac and I remain set in our stance, our guns raised and aimed at the back wall of the antechamber we're currently stuck inside. He points to the placard to the right of the joint of the wall. "If yer game, try yer finger magic on that panel and see what happens."

"What makes you think anything will happen?"

"Weel, if it wasn't Tundra or Dune who released the door, there's a good chance it might've been you."

"But I didn't do anything."

"Maybe not. Or maybe the fact that yer Elbirfae or Amberloq did somethin' without yer knowledge. After all, this compound was built by yer kind and yer realm is peppered with magic and magical folk."

I draw a deep breath. "And if it *was* me, and there *is* a door here, you're putting me right in front of the opening with something or someone on the other side."

"More likely the people who rushed out of here in such a hurry left things in disarray. The sound we heard could've been a tipped chair that fell or any number of things. In any case, we could get out of here and that's what ye want, aye?"

"It is, but…"

"I'll not let anything happen to ye, lass."

Despite his reassurance, I'm sure he wouldn't lose any sleep if something *did* happen to me. "I honestly don't think I did anything."

"Then we've got nothin' to lose. Get well over to the side and give it a try."

"Wait on us, Mac," Brody says, his tone strained.

Another shuffle behind the far wall has me glaring over at him. "That was not a tipped chair falling."

"Aye, lass. Agreed." Mac is fully focused on the wall in front of us and if we hadn't just heard the noise behind it twice, I would never have known there was anything back there.

"Do you really think this wall opens somehow?"

"That panel with those Amberloq symbols and runes are there for some reason."

He's right. It is a strange place for there to simply be a touch panel.

"Brody? Any luck opening the door to get us out of here?" I ask.

"No. None. Tundra and Dune are working on it now to see if it's an Amberloq biometric issue. They've also called for Princess Honor. Several of her security areas have been tagged to Thornebane genetics."

"Valorous was her aunt," Mac says. "She might have had a master override built into the system."

"Honor didn't open the door to this room," I say.

"No, she didn't—"

Mac's head whips up as the wall shifts and slides out of the way. The opening to the next room is filled in an instant. Three naked males rush forward and dive into the air.

"Incoming!" Mac fires two shots before one of the attackers

soars over the console and the other two come at us from either side.

As the male approaches, I swing the weapon, tracking him, but I've never seen a man move so fast. His hand juts out and a solid strike knocks the gun from my grip.

I raise my guard but I'm not fast enough.

He backhands me across the face and my head snaps back. My muscles tense and then I'm fighting with all I have.

The antechamber was small before but now with five warriors battling hard, there's no room to move.

He charges me, but I'm ready this time. I meet the force of his approach, bringing my knee up to aim for his goods, while swinging my wing around to attack on a second level.

He smacks my wing out of the way and I duck, trying to grab his wrist and crack my other wing into his face. He catches it easily and I curse.

He's so, slecking fast.

I twist and ram my knee into his side, and he grunts and grabs my hair. Another hard strike to my jaw spins my head to the side.

Pain burns hot on my cheek, and blood sprays between us and across his face.

He flicks his tongue along his lip, capturing my blood in its path. The growl that tears from the base of his throat is like nothing I've ever heard before.

His gaze narrows on me.

That one moment of hesitation is a gift I won't waste. Extending my claws, I bring my wing around and catch him in the ribs, knocking him back.

The male has a golden sheen to his skin, his body chiseled with angular beauty. Broad shoulders, trim waist, strong arms. If he wasn't trying to rip my head off my shoulders, I might swoon.

As it is, if I swoon it will be from head trauma.

When I charge him, my gaze locks with his rich, honey-gold eyes.

Get. Off. Me.

I think the words with all my might and watch as his pupils dilate. He snarls and shakes his head as if he's feral. Reaching with the speed of a viper, his fingers tighten around my throat and the path of oxygen is blocked.

The pressure in my skull builds and if I don't get free, he's going to strangle me.

Lifting my knee, I aim for his groin, but he shifts so all I manage to hit is the solid muscle of his thigh. I try to headbutt him, but all that accomplishes is spraying more blood from my lip onto his face.

I bring my wing around hard and crack him in the temple. The blow knocks him sideways, and he crashes into the wall face first. I take the brief moment of his distraction to get reacquainted with breathing.

Mac fires his weapon twice more and the metal projectiles ricochet around us. I call my wings around me as a shield and push through the opening in the wall into the next room.

It's a medical laboratory of some kind.

Five containment cylinders stand against the wall. Three are empty, and two have tall, winged soldiers still in stasis sealed inside.

A feral growl behind me brings me around to all three of our attackers converging on Mac.

I don't like the guy much, but three on one isn't sporting. Besides, he was decent to me while we were trapped in that room.

Searching for a weapon isn't a problem, there's a wall of them in a display rack. I rush forward grabbing a pain stick for my left hand and unsheathe my blade for my right.

"Get off him, assholes." I come in swinging, but another of

the golden boys turns. He simply raises his hand and catches both my wrists without effort.

The contact of skin on skin sends a jolt of energy through me and I have to lock my knees to keep from ending up on the ground.

He shoves me off and I stagger into the third one. The male spins me and wraps a steel arm around my throat from behind.

"Stop this!" I gasp. "Just stop!"

The one who tossed me turns his gaze, his eyes wild. He leans closer, his lip curled in a cruel smile. "Say that again."

I unleash the fury in my words and meet his aggression with my own. "Stop this, now!

~

Mac

I let off a roar of fury and release my beast, freeing the giant, red battle cat within. Unlike wildling shifters that can transform at will and in the blink of a moment, for me, transition between forms is both slow and painful.

Not as painful as getting majorly ass-beaten by three genetic freaks trying to use me as a punching bag, but almost as bad.

Bones snap, muscles stretch, and ligaments tear.

The fiftieth time is as bad as the first.

It always sucks.

With a feral roar, I drop to the floor, flip onto my back, and use all four paws to tear at their flesh. I manage to back them off, but their skin seems enhanced for strength and barely affected.

Still, their re-evaluation of the situation gives me the chance to lunge. Me launching from the ground to six feet in the air seems to catch them off guard. My canines sink deep into the fleshy muscle of a male's collarbone, and I take the fucker to ground.

The wash of blood sings in my veins and everything about the moment starts to tingle.

I have no idea what kind of magic they've been infused with or what their molecular composition consists of, but that ain't right.

And you know what else ain't right?

Beating the snot out of a female fer no reason.

Shaking my head as I back away, I release my fangs and pounce on the darker skinned one. They're all shades of golden tan but they're definitely different tones. One is honey gold, the one that beat on Lark is flaxen gold, and the one I got a taste of is more like the gold of fire.

Pulling my teeth back, I let off a long, low snarl.

Fire Boy crouches low, his hands poised at his side, anticipating my charge. He snarls right back.

His friend is searching for a way to flank me. *Not gonna happen, mate.*

"Who are you?" Fire Boy asks.

I lift my nose to the air and draw his scent deep into my system. There's equal parts curiosity and determination. There's also a trace of fear and disorientation.

While I have no reason to trust them, nothing will be resolved with me in this form.

I take a chance and return to my human form. "Looks like now I'm one of the nakey warriors club, lads. Ye owe me a uniform."

The three men have ceased their aggressions and are standing there looking angry and confused.

"Dial back the hostilities, boys," Lark says. "We're not your enemies. Talk to us and we'll sort this out without more bloodshed."

"Who are you?" Fire asks again, shifting his gaze from me to her and then back again.

"I'm Lark, General of the Forested Jungle Biome, and that's Connor MacDougall, commander of the military squad sent to secure this building for the Crown of Dornte."

"Did Lady Valorous send you?" Flaxen asks, his body language hyper-focused on Lark.

"No," I say, shaking my head and drawing his attention away from her. "Valorous Thornebane was killed by the Usurper Queen Laryssa two years ago. She has recently been defeated and the realm is now back under Thornebane rule."

"If Lady Valorous is truly dead, who sent you?" Fire asks.

I spot a stack of fatigues in the next room and point. "How about I explain while we cover the jewels and give the lady some respect?"

They don't seem to understand. "Never taught the concept of modesty, I take it. Or would that be a genetic integration?"

They say nothing, so I ease past them with my hands at the ready and make my way to the supply shelf. Grabbing a pair of gray fatigues, I step into them and conceal the raging battle cock I'm sporting. "Now then, that's better, aye?"

They don't seem bothered either way.

They also seem to have gone back to being silent.

"You mentioned Valorous coming fer ye. Does that mean ye know who and what ye are?"

They look from me to Lark but say nothing.

Lark sighs. "Answer us. We're trying to help you."

Flaxen straightens but does not meet her gaze. "We are the failed attempt at creating elite genetically enhanced soldiers."

"Failed attempt?" I repeat, eyeing them up and down. Okay, that's not something I can unsee. I focus on lifting my gaze. They are still very naked, and it seems genetic soldiers also get adrenaline erections and apparently genital enhancements.

I take a guess at judging their sizes and grab three more pairs of pants from the shelving rack. "What do ye mean failed attempt?"

I toss them each a pair and they snag them out of the air without shifting their gaze away from Lark. Their reflexes are sharp, and I have the sense they're assessing and calculating everything around them.

"We were decommissioned and put into stasis due to an inability to engage."

I laugh. "Ye didn't seem to have any deficiency in that arena. When that wall opened, ye engaged just fine. Try again."

"Not physical engagement," Honey gold says.

"What kind of engagement are you talking about then?" Lark asks.

"Our genetic enhancements didn't engage."

Lark looks at me, but I've got nothing. I point to the other two still in their stasis cylinders. "What about them?"

"They were the alpha and beta prototypes. They failed to engage as well."

The door to the far corridor opens on the other side of the antechamber and Tundra, Dune, Brody, Lukas, and every member of Alpha Squad come flooding in.

The golden boys, turn and tense but I raise my hand. "Hold! Everyone hold yer positions."

CHAPTER FIVE

Link

I block the female from the incoming forces and my brothers ready to attack. The feline male shouts to hold and the bodies flooding into the outer room hesitate, seemingly to consider obeying the command.

"Don't make this worse than it is," the ebony-winged female says to us. "Stand down. I swear we aren't the enemy."

Every instinct within me wars with her request, but I can do nothing but hold my position.

Everyone freezes in place as well.

The male raises a hand to the incoming force, but his attention is focused on us. "Princess, please remain where ye are. We haven't determined the allegiance of these men. I don't want ye in the line of battle."

Allegiance?

"They attacked you, Mac." A blond Elbirfae warrior states, studying the evidence of our battle scattered around the room. "That's not a good sign for them being on Team Thornebane."

"Let me pass." The female Elbirfae grips my shoulder to turn me out of her path. The contact is both superficial and invasive at once.

As she passes my hip, she glances down, and then meets my gaze. Her pupils dilate and she swallows before speaking. "You boys need to cover your cocks before you're flashing Princess Honor and her mates take offense."

Despite me having no interest in pleasing her, I step into the pants the male provided us and do as she says. It's maddening to feel compelled to follow her commands. "Why would me being or not being clothed offend the princess and her mates?"

The female's gaze narrows on mine, and she draws a deep breath. "You're serious."

"Of course."

She seems unable to answer my question and points to the clothing. "Just trust me. All of you."

My brothers do as commanded, the tension in their frames suggesting they are equally annoyed at being coerced into compliance.

What is forcing us to comply?

"It's like they're synchronized," a female soldier says. "If I'm right, this data reader will tell us which units they are and what we're dealing with."

"Stay where ye are, lass," the male says, reaching for the device. "Give it here and walk me through it."

He takes possession of the data reader and moves to address my brother. "Do ye know what this is and what it does?"

"Affirmative."

"I'm gonna scan ye and yer not gonna try anythin', are we clear?" The male looks over to the female in uniform and dips his chin. "What now, lass?"

"From what I learned from their schematics, at the nape of their neck, there is a data chip inserted into a spinal port. That's the reader. It should tell you which unit you're dealing with and what its specialties are."

"*Its* specialties?" another female says from the back. "I think it's safe to say him or his. Even from here, I got an eyeful."

The female who presented the device experiences a five percent deepening of skin coloration. "Up here too, Princess."

The male with the auburn hair faces us, his mouth curled up at the sides. As he steps in front of me, my analytics flash an information overlay into the vision of my right eye. *Eighteen percent human. Ten percent fae. Seventy-two percent feline Sìth.*

The male arches a russet brow and holds my gaze. "Now, I'll thank ye not to bite, fight, or fuss with me."

"You need not thank me. However, if you wish for me to comply, you will allow me and my brothers to smell the princess."

His mouth quirks more noticeably. "I'm sorry... what's that now?"

"Before I allow you to scan my schematics, I would like to smell Princess Thornebane. You speak of Lady Valorous' death and of your group being a force for the Dornte Crown and yet you offer no assurance."

He shakes his head. "That's not how this works, Flax. Yer property, not people."

I consider the truth to his statement. "Why do I offend you?"

"The idea of genetically enhanced soldiers offends me. I dinnae know ye well enough to have an opinion on ye personally."

Movement in the bodies in the antechamber attracts my attention. I study the jostle of beings, assessing the level of threat.

"Let me through, boys." The female's voice contains command, frustration, and kindness.

The soldiers part to allow a tall female with silver hair to pass to the front. The moment her position places her before us, the two Elbirfae warriors step before her and open their wings and a third male raises his palms.

It's the magic of the third that poses the greatest threat of the unknown.

I assess his intentions. He is calm yet calling magic to his aid, readying for battle. The comment of the female earlier about the princess replays in my data core.

"These are your mates."

Shielded by two layers of Elbirfae wings, she grips the spine of their mighty appendages and exhales. "Correct. These are, indeed, my mates. Now, is all this fuss necessary?"

"Yes!"

The word echoes from the mouth of every person in both rooms at once.

The Princess' mouth turns up and though she shakes her head, there is no trace of frustration. "Fine, then escort me closer, so we can prove our point."

The three move as one, two screening the female as she approaches, one ready to launch an offensive.

When they stand directly before me, I step closer. "Your wrist."

The tall Elbirfae with the white wings and ebony hair growls. "You will *not* touch her."

"I need not touch her to assess her lineage. Her scent will allow me to discern if she shares the familiar markers of her aunt and the Thornebane blood."

"She does," the blond Elbirfae with beige and brown wings says.

The female with silver hair lifts her arm over the barricade of her protectors, and I lean forward. Drawing her scent deep into my system, I begin the analysis of her familial markers.

"Confirmed. You are Honor Thornebane."

"Yes, I am. My aunt began this program and I only recently found out about it. We're here today to assess the status and determine the viability of what's been happening here. Are you able to help us with that?"

I glance to my brothers. "We are not. It has been six-hundred and twenty-four weeks since we were decommissioned and only just awoke."

"That's twelve years," the male with magic glowing in his fingers says. "They turned you off twelve years ago?"

"According to the synchronizing of my internal time calculations, yes."

"And ye woke up at the exact time we entered the antechamber..." the first male says. "That seems highly unlikely to me, Flax."

"However unlikely, my account is accurate."

The blond Elbirfae seems to find amusement with my explanation. "Yeah, I think we're calling bullshit on that one, champ."

"Not necessarily," the magic user says. "If these three were activated before Brass or the other soldiers took their leave, they could've been left here to slow us down or stop us from following."

"I know nothing about that."

"Aye, so ye say," the one they call Mac says.

I meet his gaze. "Regardless of what you believe, I speak the truth. We woke only moments ago with a directive to defend the base against infiltration flashing in our information overlays. It was a direct order and we responded as such."

That seems to spark interest from several of them but it's the magical mate of the princess who speaks. "Is that something that would be programmed directly, or could that be done remotely?"

I consider his question. "If the specialist had the proper access, either is possible."

"What are you thinking, Lukas?" the princess asks.

He looks at us and then scans the stasis cylinders holding Alpha and Beta. "I'm thinking if someone woke them remotely, there is a working server somewhere we might be able to find and hack into."

"Aye, and if there's a remote server in a cloud somewhere, we might be able to figure out who left here in such a rush and what they took with them," Mac says.

The female soldier in the black tactical uniform says, turning to leave, "If there's something, I'll find it."

"Speaking of finding things," a male says from the crowd. "Drix and Blue caught sight of a vehicle and followed. They are assuming watch and have sent coordinates for us to join them."

"Aye, then let's not dally. Who's comin' and who's not? Make it quick, people, we've got men on their own out there."

CHAPTER SIX

Lark

*B*ig surprise. As Mac and a group of soldiers gear up and go, no one even pretends to consider me being included in the forward offensive. That's fine. After our initial meetup with the three super soldiers, I've had all the excitement I need for one afternoon.

I don't mind sitting out.

The three are escorted into a secure room with a clear observation window and are asked to take a seat.

Honor and I take our positions on the opposite side of the reinforced glass and are left with three, heavily armed soldiers and Lukas to watch over us.

"I'm sorry about this, boys." Honor has her finger on the speaker button and meets their gazes through the glass. "I want to trust you, but this is new to everyone, and trust is earned over time."

"They don't seem too put out," I say.

She steps back from the speaker and sighs. "They don't seem to have too much emotion about the situation at all. I know how angry I was about losing two years of my life. I can't imagine being shut down for twelve."

"I know they're engineered soldiers, but that doesn't seem remotely ethical."

Honor frowns. "I'm not pleased about any of this being done in the Thornebane name. Creed and I always wondered what came between our father and his sister. We never could've imagined this."

"Well, you inherited it with the title, so what are you going to do with it now?"

"I have no idea."

The two of us sit side by side for a moment looking at the three of them sitting side by side along the table facing us.

Wearing only the pants Mac gave them, their bodies are bare and ours to inspect. There's no getting over the similarities. Not only could they be brothers, but they could also be triplets.

Each of them has golden skin, light brown hair buzzed short, caramel gold eyes, and a perfect physique. Their broad shoulders hold up a strong frame with slender hips and that delectably muscled 'V' that drops from a male's hips toward what we've already seen to be anatomically equipped torsos.

I swallow. "Wow. The scientists really went for perfection, didn't they?"

Honor chuckles beside me. "Yes, and unfortunately, seeing them like that and knowing they're sentient and reasonable makes things more difficult. I can't just order them dismantled. I can't put them back into stasis. I can't even believe my aunt approved them being left like that for so long."

"It doesn't seem right."

"Because it isn't. And despite not knowing anything about them, I feel like I owe them reparations."

Lukas comes in to join us and frowns. "Easy now, ladies. I can't have the two of you going tender-hearted here. We don't know anything about these men and while I agree being locked down for over a decade could be terrible, we don't know if it's even true or if they're playing us."

"We know they never asked to be created," Honor says. "And we know they didn't deserve to then be shelved and forgotten."

"True, but we also don't know if what they told us is the truth. They could be programmed to take you out the first chance they get. They could be plotting to fight their way to freedom. Until we get the information, we need to understand them, they are to be considered a danger and a flight risk. Am I clear?"

"Yes, dear," Honor says.

"Yes, sir." I run down the conversation from earlier back in my mind and realize something. "We got sidetracked. Mac never scanned the data chip at the back of their necks to get even the preliminary information."

"Oh, then we should do that," Honor says.

Lukas nods and leans toward the open door to speak to one of the Alpha Squad men guarding the corridor. "Can one of you go track down that data scanner Mac had in the lab?"

"Yes, sir," one of them says.

He looks back at Honor and frowns. "I don't suppose there's any chance you'll stay out here and let me talk to them without you?"

"Nope."

"Even if I stressed the dangers of being in close proximity with soldiers, we know nothing about?"

"Even then."

I chuff. "I honestly don't think they mean us any harm."

"Says the woman with a giant bruise on her face and a split lip from the fight she was in less than an hour ago."

Honor points to my face. "That's going to be purple tomorrow."

I shrug. "Nothing I haven't been through a hundred times before. Believe it or not, goblin captors don't appreciate mouthy, headstrong women trying to shove broom handles up their scrawny assholes."

Honor barks a laugh. "No. I don't suppose they would."

I glance back at the three men. "I'm not sure what I was expecting, but these guys just make me a little sad. They were created, found not good enough, and thrown away like garbage."

"I wonder if they eat," Honor says.

"They do." Lukas points to a box he set on the floor when he arrived. "We found military rations and detailed studies of their nutritional needs in the lab next door."

"Then let's start with that," Honor says, jumping to her feet. "Breaking bread is a great way to get to know someone."

"Agreed," I say, standing to join them.

Lukas draws a long breath and shakes his head before he leads us out of the room, picks up the box, and tilts his head toward the door. "Would you mind unlocking the door and joining the party, boys?"

Two of Mac's soldiers open things up for us and take positions inside, one in the far corner facing the three and one inside the door.

"Hello again, boys," Lukas says, striding directly into the center of the space to set the box on the table. "No sudden movements, please. I'm bringing the ladies in so we can talk and have a few words, but I'm expecting you to be cool, so I don't have to ruin both our days, understood?"

The three of them look blank.

"Did you understand him?" I ask.

"No," the one who speaks the most says. Mac calls this one Flax. He's the one who I fought with, and I genuinely don't think they understand subtlety or sarcasm.

"Lukas said not to advance on us, or he'll be forced to decommission you once again."

The three of them meet my gaze. "Understood."

"And you agree not to hurt us?"

"We agree."

Lukas opens the flaps of the box and pulls sealed cellophane pouches of food rations out to set on the table. "I'm assuming, now that you're out of stasis, you'll need to eat."

They look to me.

"Are you hungry? Twelve years in stasis is a long time without food."

"Yes. There is a lack of nutritional value in our systems. Consuming four to six thousand calories per day is recommended to refuel our bodies from this state."

Honor's brows arch. "That's quite the carb load. Okay, then we better figure this out quickly because that's a lot of food and I'm not sure what the caloric load is for military rations."

The three stare down at the packs, their expressions blank.

"Go ahead." I gesture to them. "Help yourself."

"We cannot accept food or drink in a hostage or hostile detainment situation."

I sigh. "Hey. We're just talking here. There's no hostility as long as you don't try to smash my head through the wall again."

Flax turns his gaze to me and frowns. "We were instructed to fight and secure the bunker."

"And you have no idea who programmed that command?" Lukas asks.

Flax tilts his head to look at him but doesn't answer.

"Go ahead. This is how you earn our trust," I say. "You tell us things and we tell you things. And to prove the food is not a danger to you, I'll eat some with you. I'm starving." I spin a couple of the packages and find fruit crumble. "Now, eat up and answer Lukas's question. Who instructed you to attack us?"

Flax frowns at me. "I do not know. When my systems came online there was a directive flashing in our information overlay."

"Where is this information overlay?" Lukas asks.

"It is a digital readout projected from our data chip to appear in our field of vision."

Lukas nods. "Do you see it now?"

"We see it always."

"And this data chip feeds you information as you move through situations?"

"That is correct."

I pass each of them a meat stew package. "Okay, boys. Like this." I click the metal tab in the center of the bag and wait while the contents warm. After a minute or so, the logo on the outer package changes color from black to red. "That means the contents are warm. Now rip the top along the tear line and use the utensil provided on the side."

"You're good at that," Honor says.

"It's all we ate for two years in that compound." I use my resin fork to fluff up the fruit crumble. "See, boys, now we're just new friends having a picnic."

Once started, the three of them become ravenous. Forkful after forkful of stew is plowed into their mouths, barely slowing to chew or breathe.

I've been where they are.

I know what it's like to be so hungry it feels like the inside of your stomach is cannibalizing on itself. "Not too fast, boys, or you'll get a belly ache. There's plenty here and you can have it all."

Realizing this might take a while, the three of us watch and wait while the three of them have their fill.

Mac

While I change into a backup uniform, Brody drives the all-terrain vehicle and follows what the locals consider a road in this part of the quadrant. We wouldn't be able to navigate the coordinates, if it weren't for the assistance of Dune and Tundra leading the way from above.

"Whoever took off from that bunker left in too much of a hurry to know who we are," I say.

Brody leans closer to the steering wheel and looks up to the sky to see where our Elbirfae guides are leading us. "Maybe Andras Brass simply realized the bunker was compromised and evacuated to keep from having his genetic research taken into enemy hands."

"Other than the corrupt one-percenters who tried to undermine the royal order of the Thornebanes, I'm not sure who the enemy would be, lad. Besides, that's neither here nor there."

By the time I finish securing my blades to my thigh and am ready to get back in the game, we're coming up on the coordinates Drix and Blue sent us.

"There," Brody says, pointing over the steering wheel. "We should be able to see them as soon as we crest this next rise."

I reach forward and brace my hand against the dash as we bounce over the rocky terrain, the springs under us squeaking their protest as we close the distance to our destination. "What more do we know?"

"Nothing," Brody says, beside me. "Just that they spotted a vehicle moving at a rapid pace away from the vicinity of the compound and they pursued."

"So, it still could be some asshole who's late fer dinner and in a hurry to get home before it's cold."

"Yep. It could be the old Taco Tuesday tear."

I laugh and shake my head, trying to clear the buzzing in my skull. Ever since the battle with the three golden boys, my skin's been tingling, and my head has been playing all kinds of fun house rollercoaster rides in my mind.

"Mac? Are you okay?"

I shake my head again and wave his concern away. "Och,

sure, lad. I must've got my bell rung good durin' the beatdown. Don't worry. I'm sure it'll pass."

"Let me know if it doesn't. I don't want you storming the walls if you're not one hundred percent."

"Yes, dear."

Link

My brothers and I eat in silence, replenishing our nutritional requirements to bring us back within optimal operating parameters. When my readings indicate to cease nutritional input, I stop.

"Better?" Lady Honor asks.

I assess my waning hunger and nod before glancing to Shift and then Flash. They, too, are satiated. "Yes, Princess. We are much improved."

"Would it be all right if I ask Lukas to scan your data chip to record the information?"

"Yes, Princess."

She meets the gaze of the man to her left and he collects the data reader.

"Is this considered rude or offensive to you?" Princess Honor asks.

"No, Princess."

The female Elbirfae we fought with lays her hand over my wrist. Having a full data bank on social interactions, I know the contact is meant to offer comfort.

It does not.

The moment her skin connects with mine, my mating instincts come online, and I want to claim her body. This is an inappropriate impulse at an inappropriate time.

I initiate a self-diagnostic scan and ease my hand back into my lap.

"Why are you growling?" she asks.

I blink and assess her question, cutting off the vocalization rumbling at the base of my throat. "I didn't realize. That was unintentional."

"So, you're not going to launch into another tirade and try to slam us into the walls?" The subtle upturn of her mouth and the softness of her voice indicates teasing and amusement.

I am not amused. "I have no such intentions."

The quiet sound of the data reader registering coincides with my data input refreshing in front of my vision and noting I have been scanned.

"Call sign, Link: communications specialist, voice analysis, and negotiations."

I turn my head slightly to the side as the male with magic repeats the scan on my brothers.

"Call sign, Shift: molecular realignment, healing, and restoration."

Shift gives him a curt nod. "Or so they believed."

The human proceeds to access the last of us and poises the reader over my brother's data port. "Call sign, Flash: thought transference, data processing, and intel retrieval."

My brother dips his chin. "But our genetic enhancements failed to engage."

Lukas nods. "Do you know what went wrong?"

"Dr. Brass could not identify the catalyst to engage the enhancement traits."

"So, they're in there, but you simply haven't been able to activate them to access them yet."

"Correct."

"Is the catalyst something external?" Lukas asks. "And if so, as they were essentially constructing you, why wouldn't they fabricate the catalyst into the genetic components?"

"I cannot say."

"Did they believe your catalyst might still present itself in time?"

"I cannot say."

The male seems perplexed and displeased. "If you'll excuse us, soldiers, I'd like to find Josie and read the full download. Ladies? Shall we?"

When Lady Honor moves to join her mate, I set my hand over the wrist of the Elbirfae female. "Will you stay? We have questions."

The brow of the male pinches, the facial expression indicating disapproval. "We'll be back shortly. You can ask your questions then."

"Our questions are not for you. They are for her." Flash indicates the ebony haired Elbirfae.

"Her name is Lark," the Princess says. "Please address her appropriately."

Flash offers the princess a smile. "Our questions are for Lady Lark."

"I'd be happy to stay," Lark says.

The downturn of the male's mouth indicates his disapproval continues. "Fine. I'll leave the guards."

"Our questions are of a private nature," I say.

"Tough shit. There's no way you're getting Lark alone in a room. The guards stay."

"What about one guard on the outside of the door and another on the other side of the viewing window," Lark suggests.

Lukas shakes his head. "No deal. This isn't a democracy. The guards stay."

"I'm sure I can manage—"

The male doesn't even consider her response. He's halfway out the door when he replies. "Humor me."

When he and Princess Honor leave, the female sits at the table to speak to us. "All right. What are your questions?"

CHAPTER SEVEN

Lark

$\mathcal{A}$s my question floats out to the three soldiers, their gaze grows intense and their heads all tilt to the side as if it's a practiced and synchronized movement. Link reaches forward, slowly, and I get the impression he's trying not to frighten me or have me shrink back.

He's in luck. I don't scare easily.

Of the three, he's the most intense. He has a perma-pissed off expression that makes him seem angry and unapproachable.

Lifting his hand from the table, his fingers brush the split in my lip and then he presses hard enough to come away with blood from the wound.

I blink and hiss inwardly, but I'm careful not to react. Instead, I watch him, trying to understand what's going on in his mind.

Turning in his seat, he holds one finger out and offers it to Flash. "Taste her blood."

Flash leans forward and sucks one of Link's fingers into his mouth. His cheeks hollow as he closes his eyes. It's an extremely homo-erotic gesture.

I try to keep my mind from wandering and wondering... They call themselves brothers but is that a sibling kind of bond or more a brothers-in-arms relationship? I saw their physical attributes but are their cocks cosmetic to allow them to seem more humanoid or are they fully functioning?

I draw a deep breath and continue watching Flash suck Link's finger. Who am I to judge? They are both beautiful males and have been down here abandoned by their makers for over a decade.

What happens in the creepy science bunker stays in the creepy science bunker, right?

Flash eases back and then turns to me. His tongue glides over his bottom lip and he swallows. He studies my face, his expression intense. "Interesting."

"What's interesting?" I ask, my throat dry.

Flash doesn't answer.

Link offers Shift the other finger. Without a word, the soldier at the end of the table leans across Flash to suck my blood into his mouth the same way his brother did.

The moment Shift's lips close over the digit, he closes his eyes and moans. I'm not sure whether to be turned on or creeped out.

Who am I kidding—I'm both.

I swallow, trying to rein that in. Sure, these guys have been built to the specifications of perfect male specimen but less than an hour ago they were naked and kicking my ass.

I'm not sure why I added the *naked* part, but after seeing them in full frontal glory, it seems to bear mentioning.

"You find us sexually stimulating." Shift's head tips to the side.

I let off a laugh. "Don't flatter yourself."

"My assessment is accurate and yet it angers you. Why?"

"Because you're wrong."

"Your pupils are dilated, your breasts swelled, and your core body temperature is rising, bringing a flush of pigmentation to your cheeks."

"Her hormone and pheromone levels have changed as well," Link says. "It is definitely arousal."

I close my eyes and draw a deep breath. "Please don't do that."

"Do what?" Link asks.

"Don't analyze me and announce your findings. It's rude and it's embarrassing."

Flash frowns. "It's a simple declaration of biological facts. Why is that rude?"

The question is genuine, his expression both curious and confused. "I am a soldier. When I sit before you among my fellow soldiers, I am not a female, and I am not supposed to react to people around me in any sexual nature."

"Biological attraction is a non-conscious response to stimuli," Shift says, joining the conversation. "There is nothing you can do to control it."

"Maybe not, but it's considered polite not to notice when it's inappropriate and involuntary."

"Like how when the feline male cloaked his erection downstairs, and you averted your gaze until he was clothed?"

I swallow, cursing the heat burning my cheeks. "Yes, like that."

The three of them seem to consider that.

Before they can launch into another round of questions about pheromones and erections, I tap my throbbing lip. "You tasted my blood and found it interesting. Why?"

Shift and Flash look to Link and he answers. "During our altercation, the spatter of your blood entered my mouth. From that moment, your command seems to have overridden my programmed directive to battle to secure this facility. You commanded me to stop, and I stopped despite my intentions to the contrary."

I take a moment to let that sink in. "How would what I say overwrite your programmed directive?"

"It could not. Or, at least, it *should* not."

"And what about you two?" I ask, meeting the gazes of Shift and Flash.

"It was the feline male for me." Shift caresses his collarbone and the teeth marks where Mac's fangs pierced his golden flesh. "There was a transference of magical essence and I felt both aroused and compelled to submit to him."

Link nodded. "It was the same for me with her."

I skip right over the aroused part of the declaration and glance to Flash. "What about you?"

He shakes his head. "I submit to my brothers. When they stood down, I did as well."

Well, isn't this interesting?

I return my attention to Link. "And why did you have them taste my blood?"

"To assess their opinions and reactions. I thought, perhaps, this is another deficiency in my construction and wanted my brothers' opinions."

"You think this makes you defective?"

He dips his chin. "Of course. We were built as elite soldiers. If a drop of an opponent's blood can override my directives, bring my mating impulses online, and make me submit to their commands, I am most definitely ineffective as a soldier."

I read the confusion in his caramel eyes and although this is horribly awkward and Lukas' guards are getting way more than they bargained for, I feel bad for the guy. "I'm sorry."

"Why would you apologize? The shortcoming is not your doing."

"No, but I know what it's like to be deemed less of a soldier because of something out of my control. In my case, I am female."

Shift tilts his head. "What does gender have to do with being a soldier?"

"That's a good question, but one for another day. The fact is... it *is* a discriminating factor. I am the first female Amberloq in the history of this quadrant and everyone is watching me and waiting for me to fail."

"They believe you are deficient?" Link asks.

"In a sense, yes."

"I do not. You fought me with admirable strength, coordination, and determination. Your only deficiency is the level of your training."

Ouch. That stings.

But unlike everyone else who has thrown that at me today, he doesn't mean it as a slight. He's simply evaluating and stating his assessment.

"So... back to the three of you tasting my blood. What did that tell you?"

Link smiles at me and I feel a soft flutter in my mind. It's a subtle nudge, a breeze through my thoughts and then I feel his presence gaining strength.

No, not just him... I feel all three of them.

Link's gaze narrows on mine. There's a subtle pop of tension in my head and then he tilts his head and grins. *From the moment I came into contact with your blood, my system has been unlocking and awakening new power and abilities. It's the same for my brothers as well. You, Lady Lark, are our catalyst.*

Mac

"Alpha Squad, get inta position." I give the order and my squad moves in from the front and the back of an old barn standing on the outskirts of a small village. The place is ninety percent surrounded by dense trees and if the boys hadn't tracked the truck by air, I doubt we'd have ever found it.

The truck Drix and Blue spotted racing away from the Amberloq bunker drove straight here and straight inside. With it being a large box truck, there's no way to know who was inside or how many.

There's also no way to know how many were inside when they arrived.

"Alpha-3 and 8 in position."

"Alpha-4 and 9 in position.

Mac nodded. "Alpha-1, 2, and 5, moving in."

Brody, Tazz, and I approach the back door of the barn and I give Tazz the nod to go. He presses his hand to the barn door, closes his eyes, and then...*Boom!*

The sonic pressure that boy can push from his palms is incredible.

The barn door shatters, and Brody and I rush forward giving our boy a moment to get his gun in hand and follow.

The sound of our forced entry signals the other two groups to advance. The clatter of wood falling to the dirt and stone ground inside the barn is the only response from the inside we get.

Swinging my aim from shadowed corners to the loft above to the stalls down the stable corridor, I search for evidence of our prey.

"Clear," Brody snaps from ahead.

"Clear," Martin calls from the back.

"Clear, Tazz says, leaning over the loft rail above.

"How the fuck did they ghost us, boys?" I snap. "Tear this place apart and get me some answers."

"I've got a body," Dwa shouts looking into the window of the truck. "Make that two."

Shit. I jog around the truck to get a look.

"No need to rush a rescue, lads. Their necks are very definitely broken. We'll back up and give ye room to assess the truck."

"Got it," Dwa says.

I step out of his way while he circles the tin box and then rolls beneath it to scan for—

"It's hot! *Fall back!*"

"Fuck! Ye heard the man, lads. Pull back!" I barely get the words out when the world explodes into a fiery ball of hell.

The truck lifts off the ground, metal screaming as it twists and shatters behind a wave of detonation. It picks me up off the ground and throws me back like I weigh nothing.

I hit the support post of the barn and feel my bones shatter inside me. Dropping to the floor with a thud, my head rings as my vision fails. My cat writhes to take control but my bones won't withstand the stress of transformation.

It will kill me for sure.

I canna lose consciousness... not when my men are in trouble.

I spot Dwa in the field of burning debris and pull myself across the dirt to clasp his hand. The soldier is not long for this realm. His lower half has been blown off and there's no comin' back from an injury like that.

"I think I'm in trouble, Mac," Dwa sputters, blood leaking out of his mouth.

"Och, don't go there, my brother. Close yer eyes and know I'm here with ye."

"It's been an honor, sir."

"Fer me as well, lad." A shearing pain in my side is pulling for my attention, but I've got none to give. I hold Dwa's gaze, unblinking until the light of life extinguishes in his eyes.

"Fuck, Mac, we..." Brody drops to his knees next to our fallen friend. "Dwa?"

"He's gone."

"Fuck."

"Tazz is down," Martin shouts somewhere over the field of fire. "Can I get some help over here?"

Brody curses. "Fuck. I saw him thrown from the loft. I bet he's busted up bad."

"Take this." I reach into the pocket of my pants and hand Brody the vial of phoenix tears I keep for emergencies. "I'm right behind you."

Brody takes the vial and narrows his gaze on me. "You okay, Mac?"

"Yeah. Just got the wind knocked out of me and wanted to be with Dwa."

"Anyone?" Martin shouts over the burning skeleton of the truck.

"Go." I wave my hand and move like I'm rolling to my feet. "Make sure he's all right."

Brody takes the tears and rushes off.

I groan and fall flat on my back. If my second in command knew I was busted up too, there's no question who he'd force those tears on... but my men are my priority.

"Mac!" Dune rushes over and flaps his wings to clear the smoke to scowl down at me. "Slecking hell, what are you doing having a dirt nap? Now is not the time or the place."

I cough, blood sputtering through my lips. "Sometimes ye fight and others ye chillax."

My voice is all wrong and we both know it.

He takes a closer look at me and curses.

"Reality is messy, my friend. It's all right fer the captain to go down with the ship. There's honor in that."

With a curse, he scoops me off the dirt floor and I brace

against the searing pain. I cry out, but my agony is absorbed by the vicious crackle and hiss of the fire around us.

The barn is old, and the wood is dry. It's going up like a brushfire consuming its prey.

"I've had enough of this slecking inferno. Take a deep breath."

I do as I'm told and then he's pushing back the way we came. The back entrance is consumed by flames. Smoke stings my eyes, but there's nothing to be done about that.

The crackling of wood and the snapping of beams above me has my heart pounding. "This whole feckin' place is about to come down."

Flexing his wings, Dune shields us from the heat as he searches for the other exit. The brilliance of the flames hurts my eyes, but not as much as the smoke.

A loud crack sounds above us.

"The support beam is burning through. When that happens, the roof will cave in and we'll both be buried and burned alive. Ye need to leave me and get out."

"Not gonna happen."

Crack.

Dune looks up and dives out of the way as a section of the roof comes crashing down.

Flaming wood collides with his back and he staggers to remain on his feet. The jostling is excruciating and I'm not sure if it wouldn't be better to lay down and die. The smoke is thick, making breathing almost impossible. It feels like my lungs are on fire.

Dune gathers himself and flaps his wings once more, allowing us to take a few breaths.

Another crack above signals the coming collapse of the entire structure. Dune looks up, gathers me tighter into his arms, and launches toward the inferno above.

The two of us are engulfed in flames and the pain triples. I'm not going to even try to fight.

I let the pain take me to oblivion.

CHAPTER EIGHT

Lark

$\mathcal{I}$'m both skeptical and embarrassed as I relay Link's revelations to Honor and Lukas. "And although it's awkward, I think them having an attachment to me could be a good thing."

Lukas narrows his gaze on me. "I have my own thoughts on that, but why do you think so?"

"Well, if I am their catalyst and somehow the enzymes in my blood unlocked their warrior traits, it's good to have an off-switch to control them."

"*If* you're the catalyst *and* they truly are bound to listen to you, I would agree," Lukas says.

Honor frowns. "What? You don't think they're telling the truth?"

Lukas shrugs. "I'm not sure what to think yet. It's early days. We don't know anything about those three men. Maybe they've been above board and are telling us the truth or maybe they're fantastic liars and are infiltrating our ranks by gaining our trust. We came into this operation to shut things down."

Honor sighs. "I know, but that was before I sat there and spoke to them. They might be a little stilted and bioengineered, but in the state they are in now, they are sentient soldiers. I can't just turn them off because the idea of all this offends me."

"It seems Brass, or whoever was in charge here, didn't share that view, babe."

She shakes her head. "The fact that they sat idle in those cylinders for twelve years is horrific. Were they aware? I know what it's like to be locked in my mind while everything around me is a void of nothing. I won't allow that to happen to them again."

Lukas looks frustrated with her stance. "What if they turn out to be a danger to Creed and the Crown of Dornte?"

"That's different. If they turn on us, they'll be treated like any enemy coming at us would. I don't think that's where this is headed."

Lukas looks from her to me and frowns. "You two are too compassionate to be objective."

Now it's me who's frowning. "Do you think I'm that gullible?"

"No. My evaluation has nothing to do with you, Lark. The truth is three genetic super soldiers have landed in our lap. We have no idea what they're capable of or what their training or programing might be. I'm only saying we have to keep our minds and eyes open and our senses sharp."

All right. That's fair.

"So, what's our next step?" I ask.

Lukas sits on the edge of the desk and brushes a hand down the thigh of his fatigues. "Well, I'm of two minds for that. One, we take Link, Flash, and Shift back to the city and test them, working toward integration into our lives."

We certainly have enough space at Amberloq Hall and we could observe them there.

Honor frowns. "I'm not comfortable with that. It's too soon

to bring them that close to the castle. I don't want to shut them down, but I also don't want to open us up to more trouble."

He nods. "Agreed. The second option was my preference too."

I lift my chin. "And what is your second option?"

"The fifth floor of this bunker is where the science crew lived in the barracks. We could leave them here with a few security officers and observe them while we assimilate them and study the information we're gathering on the super soldier program."

My instincts take over. "I'll stay with them."

I'm not sure what Honor hears in my voice, but her expression tightens. "Why is this so important to you?"

I try to put it into words. "I feel like I understand what they are going through and believe I could help them understand our position. I also think that if I am truly their catalyst and off-switch, it would be a good idea to build a rapport with them."

Lukas frowns. "You've known them for two hours, Lark. It feels to me like you might not be objective. Maybe you are special to them or maybe they see you're having a rough time fitting into the core of this group and they're exploiting a weakness."

"Ouch. You don't pull punches, do you?"

He shakes his head. "In the business of security, honesty and expectations keep people alive. That's my goal here. To keep as many of our people alive as I can, including you."

I respect that. "All right. If you allow me to stay, I'll keep my guard up and observe them over the next while without automatically buying into their account of things. Yes, I hope they are telling the truth, but I will consider all motives and possibilities."

"That's all I'm asking."

Honor steps closer and touches my arm. "I know we're still finding our dynamic, but I don't want you to do anything you don't want to. There is no pressure here for you to take on dangers to prove anything to us. We'll build our respect and trust over time the same way as with Dune, Tundra, and Lukas."

"I appreciate that, Princess, but that's not why I want to stay."

"Then explain it to me again," she says, her amethyst eyes meeting mine without hostility or challenge.

"I am the kind of person who needs to feel useful. I strive on handling tough situations and caring for people. It's why I excelled as the leader in the goblin camp and I'm sure it's part of the reason I've had so much trouble since being rescued."

She listens and I wait for the tension to creep into her posture. It doesn't. She remains relaxed and receptive, so I continue.

"I'm sure that sounds like an ego thing, and you and others have come at me hard as if that's the case, but it has much less to do with my ego as it does with my honor. I was raised by my yamma and yumpa. So, maybe my values are outdated but I believe in working hard and being a productive part of my community."

"And you believe taking lead with the three of them will satisfy some of those needs?"

"My gut says I'm needed here."

Honor nods. "I believe in valuing our instincts. If your gut says this is your mountain, I won't stand in your way."

"Thank you, Princess."

She nods. "Thank you for trusting me enough to have a genuine conversation. I like you, Lark. I have from the beginning. I believe we will make a great team, given time to settle into our relationship."

Maybe. I've never really thought so before, but maybe things could go in a different direction.

"So, the fifth floor? Do you mind if we take a tour before the others get back."

Lukas nods. "I'll get you one of the elevator access cards Josie programed for us."

"Thank you. I'd like to get a sense—"

"Squad Leader, we've got trouble with the field team." The female soldier working on the computer systems leans into the room looking shaken. "They found two bodies on scene and moved in to investigate. There was a detonation. One dead, two critical, most wounded."

Lukas jumps up from where he's sitting on the desk and rushes toward the exit of the administration room. "Fuck. What's their ETA?"

"The two critical are being flown back by your mates and will arrive in twenty. The others are enroute in the all-terrain vehicles and will take twice that long."

"Josie? If this place is a genetic research facility there has to be a med lab of some kind, right?"

"I wanted to send Todd and Evans down to start raiding supplies, but you have them watching the three."

I shake my head. "Take the men and tend to the wounded. I'll watch the three. I'll escort them down to five and we'll take a look around. If I'm going to be here with them for a few days, there's no sense having men with guns hovering. They'll either attack me now or later."

Honor frowns. "I don't like that logic, Lark."

I shrug. "Get your med unit set up for triage. I'll keep the three out of your way."

Lukas looks at me and then Honor. "I don't like it, but we need the help."

Honor pegs me with a serious stare. "On your guard, Lark. I trust your instincts, but don't risk your own safety. If they threaten you or overpower you in any way, I want you to get out of there and lock down the floor."

"Understood, Princess, but don't worry. I've got this." I stride out of the meeting area and head back to the room we were using for interrogation. Head up, eyes forward, I test my resolve.

At least, I hope I've got this.

Link

When the female returns, she signals to the two soldiers in black fatigues to report to Lukas right away. She waits while they leave and remains in the doorway with her arms crossed over her chest. She looks as if she has something to say.

We wait to be updated.

"After speaking to the Princess and Lukas, I volunteered to take you down to the living quarters. There are still a lot of questions about you boys, but sitting in this room is unnecessary."

"I fail to understand," I say, seeking out the meaning of her comment.

"We want to believe you speak the truth, but until we do, the three of you will remain here."

"Are we to be decommissioned?" Flash asks.

"No. Oh, no, nothing like that. You will be... guests of the Princess... sort of. I will stay with you and likely another soldier or two and we will get to know you, observe your abilities, train with you, and assess what Valorous' program did to you."

"You will remain with us?" I repeat.

She nods. "If I truly am your catalyst, I think it's important to see how your abilities respond to my presence."

"You *are* our catalyst." Saying that stirs up more emotion than I understand.

"Why do you sound angry about that?"

"I don't know."

She's watching me and seems as confused as I am.

I try to elaborate. "I am pleased my enhancements are coming online but find your part in it unsettling."

"I appreciate you being honest about that because, yeah, unsettling is one way to describe it."

"Will you truly stay with us?" Flash asks.

Her gaze is warm, and all sensor readings tell me she is being genuine. "That's the plan. And unless you try to leave here without permission, attack me or one of the others, or do something that convinces us you have not been truthful, I will stay and help you figure this out. We'll do this together."

Flash nods. "We will abide by your terms."

Shift and I look at him and he shrugs. "My apologies... I cannot speak for Shift and Link. *I* will abide by your terms."

I meet Shift's gaze and read his intentions. My link to his mind might not be completely formed yet, but I can sense his thoughts more clearly by the moment.

I draw a deep breath and accept the position Flash put us in. "Flash is correct. If what you say is true, *we* will abide by your terms."

The upturn of Flash's mouth coincides with a rush of positive emotion over our mind link.

I'm not sure what to make of that. Flash is third in our hierarchy. Why would he choose now to speak for the three of us?

"So, would you like to come with me and explore our new temporary home?" she asks.

"Yes," Flash says, standing before the rest of us have a chance to respond. "Thank you, Lady Lark."

What has gotten into him?

I watch him, wondering if perhaps the catalyst's blood awoke something else in Flash other than his genetic enhancements.

The female returns his smile and lets off a melodic sound as she gestures to the open doorway. "Then let's go explore. Shall we?"

~

Flash

For the first time in my existence, I don't wait for Shift or Link to indicate what I should do. With Lady Lark, I am free. She is my catalyst and set us on a new path. Surely now that we can prove our worth as soldiers, they won't decommission us.

I hold onto that hope as we exit the meeting room and glance back to my brothers to see if they are following.

They are.

Of course, they are.

Even though what's happening to us is confusing and unclear, being awake and under the watchful eyes of Princess Thornebane and her soldiers is better than being stuck in the dark void of stasis.

"Lady Lark, when you say living quarters, what does that mean? Are we not to regenerate in our stasis cylinders?"

She leads us to the elevator and presses the call button. "I'm told there are a dozen private bedrooms downstairs with a common kitchen, lounge, and workout room. I thought we could get to know one another better down there. Unless you'd prefer your cylinders. Would you be more comfortable—"

"No!" all three of us shout in unison.

She chuckles, eyes wide. "I guess that settles that. Bedrooms it is."

The doors to the elevator slide open and she presses a badge over the scanner and keys in a code. "Is there anything about your eating or sleeping routines that I should know? Do you need to plug in or download or anything?"

I laugh and look at Link and Shift. They found that funny too. "No. We don't plug in."

The flush of color to her cheeks makes her even more compelling.

She leads the way into the elevator and the three of us step inside and end up surrounding her. Link mentioned his mating instincts coming online. Mine have as well. He worries it might be a sign of a deficiency in our programming—but he worries *everything* is a sign of deficiency in our programming.

I don't think so.

I think Lark is our catalyst because she's meant for us. There is nothing wrong with us wanting to form bonds with her.

The elevator opens and we step into the lounge area of the living quarters she told us about. Three brown leather couches sit facing a square table, and on the wall opposite, a large black screen.

The place has obviously been lived in, but is still orderly and clean.

"Have you guys ever been in living quarters before?" Lark asks.

Shift shakes his head. "No, but we have simulation information in our programming. Being an elite soldier requires blending in, merging with a crowd, and convincing people we belong there."

I nod. "We haven't had a chance to encounter situations to acquire real world experience yet, but you can help us with that."

Link brushes close to Lark and circles her. When he's standing behind her, he lifts her hair and lowers his face to inhale. "What is this scent?"

"Lenai blossom. It's my shampoo."

"It smells delicious."

Shift moves close to smell her hair and then I follow. Dipping my chin, I breathe deeply. My desire for her doubles. "And the more experiences we share, the faster we'll adapt to become more natural in social settings and activities."

Shift chuckles. "You wish to copulate with her."

I let her hair fall back against the junction of where her

ebony wings protrude from her back. "Yes. Link is not the only one who's mating instinct has activated. I wish, very much, to join with Lady Lark."

The female swallows, her cheeks flushing a deep crimson. "Look, guys, I'm flattered. Yes, you are very attractive men, but I'm not here to copulate or join or have sex with you."

"You are attracted to us." I scan her body's reactions and confirm her arousal. "You look at us and your body warms to the idea of joining with us."

"Most women you come across will have the same reaction. Whoever designed you did a very good job."

Link tilts his head. "Your mating instinct has engaged, you admit you find us attractive, and yet you deny yourself the opportunity to experience the pleasures of joining. Why?"

She chuckles and glances at each of us before looking down to her hands. "Remember how I said it was rude to analyze me and announce your findings?"

Link nods. "Yes. You said even though we recognize something to be true, it is polite to pretend we do not notice."

"Exactly. Any sexual arousal you pick up from me is involuntary and I don't want there to be any confusion. I'm here as a friend and as a fellow soldier who hopes to help you through a difficult transition."

"So, no copulating?" I ask.

She shakes her head. "No, Flash. No copulating."

"That is disappointing," I say, confused by the contradiction between her words and her desires.

Link takes a step back and scans the living area. "Very well, may we see where we will regenerate?"

Lark seems to appreciate the question. "Sure. Let's go look around."

CHAPTER NINE

Lark

Slecking hell, all this talk about copulating and being sexually aroused isn't doing me any favors. They are panty-damp gorgeous, built for battle, and looking at me like they want to strip me down and possess me.

They might be bioengineered virgins, but they must have extensive programming because slecking hell they've got the aggressive seduction thing down.

And can we find them shirts?

With all this glorious, exposed skin and the loosely fitting scrubs tenting from their arousal, I'm about to combust into a ball of lust.

And that's before we head back to the bedrooms.

I push back my body's demand and try to focus.

This isn't natural.

Whatever magic is working on them, it's working on me too. Only, I can't let it take hold of me. How would it look if my very first mission for the Princess gets muddled because I can't keep my hands to myself?

Lukas was right... I only met them a few hours ago. There's no way I should be contemplating getting naked with them. They must have some kind of bioengineered pheromones or aphrodisiac in their systems.

That's the only answer.

The corridor to the bedrooms sits behind a glass door and is visible from the living room. The hallway is wide, long, and punctuated by six gray doors on both sides.

"Any room we want?" Flash asks.

"Sure. I don't see why not. I'm sure they're all close to being the same."

"What should we do with the personal belongings of the people who were here before us?" Link asks, pointing into the first room we come to.

I follow his gesture and see what he means. Yeah, up until our arrival, it seems at least a few of the scientists or assistants lived here.

"I'll make a quick sweep of the rooms and gather anything that looks interesting. Maybe there's a journal or something that might tell us more about the scientists and the work they've been doing here."

"Which room are you choosing, Lady Lark?" Flash asks me.

"I have no idea." Flash seems to have chosen the first room he came to, so I point to the second door on the right and look inside. It doesn't look like anyone's been using it, so even better. "I'll take this one."

Shift walks across the hall. "I'll be in here."

Link chooses the first on the left opposite Flash's room. "I really don't care. This will do."

Flash disappears across the hall from Link and comes back, holding up a man's shirt. "There is a stack of clothing in here if you want something to wear, brothers."

He pushes his arms through the sleeves and pulls the fabric

down the rippled plane of his abs. The fabric clings to his muscled frame like a second skin and I have to look away.

How could a man I barely know pulling on a t-shirt have me nearly panting? This insatiable pull I feel toward them is going to get tiresome very quickly.

Maybe there's more to being their catalyst.

It has to be more than me being too long without a good slecking. There were a few stolen moments in the prison camp but with everyone cramped into two barrack buildings, there was no privacy for anything more than a quick release.

Damn. It's been years since I had a true lover.

That has to be the problem.

I just need to be bedded properly.

The three of them are staring at me and I realize my mental diatribe isn't doing me any favors. They can read my wanton and already want to explore that further. Would that really be so bad?

Maybe it could be a teaching point.

I bite my bottom lip and give myself an inner shake. I need to prove myself to Honor and the others. No matter what's working its magic on me, I make my own decisions. "I'm fine. Nothing to see here."

"You lie, female," Link says, pressing forward. "You're hungry. We all sense it."

Flash closes in next. "Your body calls to ours. You are our catalyst. It is our honor to ease you."

I swallow. "As kind as that is to say, let's continue with the tour, shall we? We're going to be living here for the next few days or weeks. I think it's a good idea for us to explore our surroundings."

And with that, I duck past Flash and make a hasty dash toward the workout area.

~

Flash

The three of us follow Lady Lark through the rooms of the fifth floor. As she told us, there are the living quarters, a training room, a recreational room, and a data console by the elevators that would be used for accessing the bunker's systems.

Unlike the smashed and destroyed port stations and data consoles we passed on our way down here, this one appears to be mostly intact.

It's damaged for certain, but not terribly so.

Of course, Link doesn't miss that observation. *Lure the female out of this area so I can assess the systems.*

Assess them for what purpose? I ask.

I feel his annoyance brushing my mind over the neuro-link he's created between us. *I want to ensure all they told us is true and to do that, I need access to the program's systems. And to do that, I need to assess if this data console is operational.*

I don't like misleading her. She said she'll stay with us unless we do something that breaks their trust. Infiltrating their computer system the first moment they leave us in a room by ourselves is exactly the kind of thing that will get us put back in stasis.

Flash, just do as I ask.

Shift breaks into the mental conversation and his mind seems as conflicted as mine. *I agree with Flash. If they are skeptical we can be trusted, they will watch us and wait to catch us doing something untrustworthy. We should wait... at least until we learn more.*

Link clenches his fists beside his thighs and sends me an angry glare. *We will learn more when I assess the data console.*

"Flash? Will you help me gather up the personal effects of the people who lived here before us?" Lark lifts a packing bin and starts toward the door to the back room.

I am torn.

I want to help Lady Lark, but the moment I leave Link alone, he will do something that will cause us trouble. Lady Lark arrives at the door and glances back to me. "Are you coming? Is something wrong?"

Go with her. Trust me brother.

I have no other choice. Forcing a smile, I rush forward to open the door for her. "No. Nothing is wrong. I'm happy to help."

Together the two of us move room to room collecting anything of a personal nature that happened to be left behind in the barracks.

"Many of these sleeping quarters are unused. Valorous' technology team must have been reduced greatly from the time we were last awake."

Lark sets two notebooks into the bin and meets my gaze. "Were there a lot of scientists here at the time you were put into stasis?"

"Yes. Technologists, biologists, designers, movement specialists, engineers…" My mind wanders to all the nameless faces that used to stare at us through shatterproof glass. "And not one of them fought to keep us activated."

Lark sets the bin down on one of the beds and reaches over to take my hand. "I know how it feels to be discarded and forgotten. I'm sorry that happened to the three of you."

"The five of us," I correct. "Alpha and Beta are still in their stasis cylinders. We should free them."

She moves the bin off the surface of the bed and sits down, patting the mattress beside her. "Do you know them or just know of them?"

I accept the invitation to sit with her and remain mindful of her body language. While there were times early today when she seemed anxious and slightly afraid of us, right now, she seems only curious.

"They were placed in their stasis cylinders prior to our creation. While we have never interacted physically, their cognitive functions, while minimal, were present in the same data cycles as ours."

"Are you saying you were aware of them even in your state of stasis?"

"Yes."

"And were they aware of you?"

"Yes."

She rubs her fingers through her long, ebony hair and the strands pick up the overhead lighting and shimmer blue. "I'll report that to Princess Honor."

I'm not sure what that means but she seems unsettled, so I leave her to her thoughts.

"You are incredibly beautiful, Lady Lark," I say after a short while. "I find you physically appealing."

She stands and I match her movement.

When the impulse overtakes me, I take her hand in mine and lift it to my mouth. With our gazes locked, I kiss her knuckles. Her skin is soft and warm and smells mildly floral.

As I straighten, she traps her bottom lip between her teeth. Her fingers tighten in mine. She no longer seems unsettled by our talk of Alpha and Beta, so I step close to her. "Do you feel the pull? It's a thrum in my blood and a warmth in my skin. I cannot explain it, but it tells me you are my match."

She swallows. "We should probably get back to your brothers."

"I don't want that right now."

She tilts her head back to look at me, her green eyes wild. "No? What do you want?"

I slide my free hand to the back of her neck and bring my mouth down on hers. Shock holds me for a racing heartbeat and then my systems adjust to the bombarding sensations.

Stiff at first, it takes a moment before she sighs and melts against my body. I kiss her with everything I'm feeling. Gratitude. Awe. Hunger. It's incredible and I never want to stop.

She pushes against my chest and breaks away, meeting my

gaze. Her breath escapes in short, shallow pants and it makes the swell of her breasts against the containment of her shirt even more enticing.

"That shouldn't have happened," she says, pressing her fingers to her lips. "I'm sorry."

"Are you? I am not. Was the kiss not good?"

She exhales a laugh and shakes her head. "No. The kiss was very good. I enjoyed it but it shouldn't have happened."

"Why? If we both enjoyed it, why did you stop?"

"I'm here to assess you, not be seduced by whatever is happening between us."

My gaze narrows on her. "But you admit something is happening."

She licks her lips and swallows. "We really need to get back out to your brothers."

Before I can argue or convince her otherwise, she turns to leave. It's only after she's on her way through the door that I remember I'm supposed to be keeping her occupied. *We're coming back.*

I'm not sure if Link heeds my warning, but we find him and Shift in the kitchen searching through the cupboards.

"Did you boys find anything good?" she asks.

"Not really," Link says, handing me a box of military rations like the ones Lukas gave us upstairs.

"Lady Lark, would you teach us how to cook?" I touch her arm and am bombarded by hot flashes of memory and emotions. Of capture. Of torture. Of desperation. Of determination.

Of concern.

Of bliss.

The first emotions are older memories. The concern is fresh and making her anxious, and the bliss—well, as she described it —that was from our kiss.

"Flash? Are you all right?"

I glance down to where her hand rests on my arm again and swallow. "Yes. It seems our physical connection continued to unlock my genetic enhancements. What happened before you came down here that has you so anxious?"

She turns her emerald gaze to meet mine. "What do you mean?"

"Something happened before you brought us here. You were concerned for the other soldiers. Did we do something wrong?"

Her gaze narrows on me. "How did you know to ask me that?"

I glance down to our point of contact. "I told you. My enhancements are coming online. Call sign, Flash: thought transference, data processing, and intel retrieval."

"Thought transference?"

"That is correct. My genetic enhancement is the ability to touch flesh and read the bioelectrical impulses which store thoughts and memories. When I touched you, I was bombarded with your concern."

She takes a moment, looking at the point where her fingers touch my arm, and then steps away to break the contact. "I prefer not to have my thoughts and memories read."

Her rejection strikes a blow, but the pain is soon replaced by fear. "I apologize for offending you. Will you decommission me?"

Her brow pinches. "No. Of course, not. It's just... I'm a private person and prefer to keep my thoughts to myself. It'll take me a minute to wrap my head around you having access to me like that. For now, try not to touch me."

Try not to touch her?

After what we just shared, there's nothing I want more than to touch her. Everywhere. All the time.

Hoping to have her accept me and my abilities was stupid. I glance at my fingers, missing the warmth of her connection immediately. "Yes, Lady Lark."

She turns to me and sighs. "Give me time to think about that, Flash. There's a lot coming at us all at once. I just need a minute, okay?"

"Okay."

"Why are you concerned about the soldiers," Link asks. "Is there something we could help with? Maybe a mission we could join to prove our worth?"

Lark shakes her head. "No. Nothing like that. Many of the soldiers you saw this morning were called away to follow the ones who abandoned this bunker. I don't have the details of what happened there, but there was a detonation of some sort and many injured were being rushed back."

"Perhaps I can help," Shift says, stepping forward.

She looks at him and her expression pinches. "What were your enhancements again, Shift?"

"Molecular realignment, healing, and restoration."

She nods. "And have your enhancements awoken like your brothers' have?"

"I believe so. I feel a release of energy in my cells and my wound from the feline male has fully healed." He points to the smooth line of his clavicle and the unblemished skin there.

"You healed yourself?"

"Unknown."

"But it healed?"

"It did."

She squares off in front of him and taps a finger against the split in her lip. "How about a practical demonstration? Can you heal this?"

"You should kiss her first," I say.

Lark looks at me and frowns. "Why would you say that?"

"Because my enhancements were coming online, but after we shared our kiss, they started activating at a much greater rate."

She waves that away. "Try without the kissing."

Shift meets the challenge in her gaze and smiles. "I would be happy to try."

Moving closer, she encourages him to touch her. With my emotions still strong and unstable, her acceptance of him after the rejection of me tests my control. No one seems to notice or care.

Of course not.

I am only Flash.

Shift reaches up to probe the injury on her lip and she offers him a look of encouragement. "Go ahead. We've got nothing to lose if you try."

Shift swallows and then nods. "I don't know how this will feel to you."

"I understand."

I read her expression, wondering if she trusts him or is merely curious. More the latter, I believe. Somehow, that makes me feel better.

I sense, more than see, when he releases his healing intention and watch in fascination as the sensual line of her lip knits back together.

Lark's intake of air is laced with surprise, but no indication of discomfort presents itself. When her lip is whole once again, Shift steps back.

Lady Lark swoons and I step in to catch her fall. The moment I am supporting her weight, I'm bombarded by her dizzied state. Remembering I am not to touch her, I release my hold and step back.

The female hits the concrete floor of the bunker and grunts. After shaking her head, she glances up at me and frowns.

"Apologies, Lady Lark. I touched you without your permission after you asked me not to. It was a momentary impulse."

Her annoyance clears and she laughs. The sound is a melodic peal of feminine joy. "I guess I deserved that. Okay, new rule. If I'm wounded or fainting and your impulse is to aid me, you may. We'll work out the thought transference awkwardness afterward."

She offers me her hand and I pull her to her feet. "Thank you, Lady Lark. I promise you discretion. I will not share or repeat anything I see."

She widens her stance and braces herself to stand. "Wow, Shift. Your power is wonderful, but it's a bit like getting tumbled head over heels in a wild wind."

"Perhaps having people sit or lay down during a healing would be beneficial," Link says.

Shift nods. "Perhaps you are right."

"The important thing is that it worked," Lark says, gesturing toward the corridor. "Come. Let's see if we can help the others."

CHAPTER TEN

Shift

The black-winged female leads us up several floors, and we emerge into a room buzzing with machines and beeping with alarms. "We're losing him," a male shouts. His hands are stained with blood to his elbows and there is a great wash of scarlet across the sheen of the silver table.

"Damn, it, Mac, you stubborn son-of-a bitch, don't you die on me." Lady Honor's human mate, Lukas, is working feverishly trying to help staunch the bleeding of the red-haired, feline male.

My feline male.

Angry possession rises inside me, and I stride through the space to close the distance.

Princess Honor turns, anguish clear in the tears streaming down her cheeks. When she sees me, her eyes widen and her hand slips toward the weapon at her hip. "What are you doing?"

Several soldiers watching from the edge of the room stiffen and shift to intercede.

I raise my hands. "I mean you no disrespect in a difficult time, but I must try to aid my male."

"Your male?" Lukas repeats, looking up from his medical ministrations. "What the fuck do you mean by that?"

What *do* I mean by that?

"His feline bit me and forced my submission. He is my superior. We are bound."

Lukas looks like he's about to argue.

"The ebony-winged female is our catalyst and unlocked my genetic enhancements. I wish only to aid in the healing of my male."

"Let him try," Princess Honor says.

Lukas frowns at the other soldier in black. "What do we have to lose?"

The soldier regards me with a sneer and curses.

After a moment of contemplation, Lukas waves me closer. "He's lost a lot of blood, has innumerable broken bones, and internal bleeding. I gave him phoenix tears to heal him—they should've taken hold by now—I've also used my magic, but the damage is too extensive."

"Phoenix tears? Is that a medical treatment?" I ask.

Lukas nods. "It is usually a slam dunk quick fix. I don't know if we got to him too late or if his genetics don't respond to them or if it's too soon. Something is keeping him from healing."

I step to the edge of the surgical table and examine the injuries. Pressing a hand to his bare chest, a surge of energy pulses from my palm and into his broken body. My scan emanates through his system and then the results return to me.

As the data uploads into the information overlay of my right eye, I realize how dire the situation is. "His death is imminent without immediate intervention."

"Then intervene," Lukas says, his tone harsh and clipped.

I read his emotions, confused by the extent of affection and fear the military leader exhibits.

The warm touch of our female turns my attention to her standing beside me. "Figure things out later. Save Mac now, please."

"Yes, Lady Lark." Refocusing on the injury of my feline male, I set to work.

As I access my newly acquired powers, it is difficult to believe that after all this time, my specialty has been realized. My brothers and I were found defective. It seems the creators were incorrect.

It was not *we* who were lacking—it was *them*.

"Lark? Do you really think he can do this?" Princess Honor whispers to our female as I work.

"His enhancements are molecular realignment, healing, and restoration. He healed the bite mark from Mac's cougar form and the damage to my lip."

"Mac is badly broken up inside," Lukas says. "Let's not lose sight of that. Even if Shift's abilities are coming online, there's a big difference between sealing a split lip and knitting half his ribs back together, unpuncturing his organs, and restoring him to full health."

"Even if it's not full health, maybe the phoenix tears will be able to take him the rest of the way," Princess Honor says.

"Maybe. Fuck, I hope so." The squadron leader steps away from the surgical area and moves to the sink to begin washing off his friend's blood. When he returns to my side, he holds himself just far enough back that he doesn't touch either of us. "Please be right about this, Shift. I know you don't know us or owe us anything, but Mac's life is important. He matters to us."

He matters to me as well.

I continue to send my healing energy into the broken body before me. I know he matters. Every possessive instinct within me tells me he must be saved. He is mine.

Link's consciousness flows seamlessly into my mind. *No brother. If he is yours... he is ours.*

~

Lark

I stand with Flash and Link by the door to the med lab while Honor, her mates, and several of Mac's squadron soldiers look on. What is it about the man that inspires such loyalty and affection? In my three or four interactions with him, he's annoyed me with his cocky smirk and his attitude of superiority.

Shit. It's unkind to speak ill of the dying.

Not that he's dying.

At least I hope he's not. After years of lying in the dark void of stasis, I'm hoping this is Shift's moment to show the realm what he's capable of. I can't say I understand his attachment to Mac, but then again, I don't understand their attachment to me either.

"How long do you think it will take before we know if it's working?" Honor asks.

Brody is hovering close to the table, watching the machines monitoring his life signs. "He's not getting worse. That's all I can say for now."

"I'll take it." Honor steps into Tundra's side and the male reads her needs and wraps his arms around her. The white-feathered Elbirfae is a stunning contrast of dark and light. His feathers are the purest white of freshly fallen snow on the mountaintop, and like the snowy owl, there are small flecks of black feathers that match his ebony hair.

He snuggles the princess into his embrace and rests his chin on top of her head. The display is unguarded, and I wonder what it would be like to seek comfort from another like that.

Is there anyone in my life I am close enough with that I would trust with my vulnerabilities?

There were a few men in the prison camp who shouldered

the safety of the other prisoners with me. That was situational, not romantic.

Is there anyone I've felt connected to like that?

No. No one. Not ever.

Glancing to the genetically engineered males at my side I wonder about the strange compulsion I feel to be close to them... to trust them... to protect them.

Part of me wants to lean into the shelter of their bodies, to breathe their scents deep into my lungs, and to press myself solidly against their muscled chests.

Flash would welcome me.

Link? I don't think he would.

They told me I am their catalyst and have unlocked their potential, but what have they unlocked in me? Is it real or have they manipulated me somehow?

"Brody, turn down the alarms." Lukas dries his arms and moves back to the table. His gaze is locked on Shift, and he holds up his hands toward Mac's body. When he holds up his palms, my pulse races and my urge to push him back is overwhelming.

"What are you doing, magic man?" Honor asks.

He opens his eyes and smiles. "Getting a sense of what Shift is doing. Everyone's magic carries a distinct fingerprint. It's like a signature. I'm getting to know Shift's signature and assessing its magical potential.

The alarms cut off altogether and Brody holds his hands up. "That wasn't me."

Lukas bends down to check the readings. "Whatever you're doing, Shift, keep at it. Mac is stabilizing."

I wonder how long Shift *can* continue. I only unlocked his healing powers a few hours ago. He can't go on indefinitely.

Sweat beads on his brow and I can only imagine how much energy this is costing him. Perfect. Now I'm not only worried about Mac, but also Shift.

I take a step further into the room. "Shift, if Mac is stable and you need to take a break, don't endanger yourself—" The scowl on the soldiers' faces cuts me off from finishing that sentence.

"He will be all right, Lady Lark." Flash's knuckles brush the back of my hand, and he sends me a reassuring smile. "He was designed for just this purpose."

Link doesn't seem to agree with Flash's optimism.

"Do you think he'll be all right, Link?" I ask.

His hands are fisted at his sides and he's grinding his teeth. "I do not know. Flash is correct...he was designed for this purpose, but he has yet to assess how much energy output it costs him for a healing of this magnitude. It is concerning."

Yes. Concerning is a good way to describe it.

"Looking much better," Brody says, smiling at the readouts on the machines Mac is hooked up to. "Martin, grab another two bags of A-pos so we can hang them as soon as the healing is over."

"Roger that."

The movement of one of the soldiers seems to stir all of the Alpha Squad back to life.

"Come on, Mac," the female soldier says.

"Fight the fight, man," another adds.

"You've got this, you stubborn ass." Brody's comment gets a few laughs, but I don't find it funny.

Are any of them seeing how pale and drained Shift is? I take another step forward and brave the disapproval of Mac's men. "You've done amazing, Shift. Please don't hurt yourself in the process."

Lukas follows my concern and frowns. "Shit. He's going down. Grab him!"

CHAPTER ELEVEN

Lark

$\mathscr{I}$'m not the closest to Shift when he collapses, but I'm the one watching him as his knees buckle and he goes down. I manage to grab hold of him before he hits the floor. Lukas and Flash are the next to close in with Link close behind them.

Lukas kneels beside me, reaching over to touch Shift and assess him with swift and practiced hands. "His pulse is strong and I'm not sensing anything physically wrong with him. I think it's exhaustion and him running out of juice."

My sigh of relief leaves me in a rush.

Thank the stars.

Flash helps me to my feet, his touch tentative and carefully placed not to cause skin-to-skin contact. I know he's trying to honor my wishes. When I'm back on my feet, he presses a comforting hand against my belt at the small of my back.

"We will take him and return to our quarters." Link lifts his brother over his shoulder. "Flash, bring Lady Lark and call the elevator."

Flash doesn't hesitate to follow the command. He gestures for me to take the lead and I check in with the princess. "We'll be downstairs if anyone needs us or if there's any news."

Honor gives me a weary nod.

The farther we get from the drama of Mac's healing, the weaker I feel. I press the button to call the elevator and lock my knees. Sure, the adrenaline of the moment is wearing off, but no one needs to see me losing my hold on things.

In the elevator, I hit the button for sub-level five and step into the back corner to stay out of their way and hopefully off their radar.

When we emerge downstairs, Link carries Shift into the bedroom he chose this afternoon and lays him on the bed.

The three of us watch him sleeping for a bit before Link turns off the overhead light and his still form is lit only by the dim glow of a desk lamp. "He won't wake until late morning at the earliest."

"Then it's just the three of us." I'm nervous about that and with their heightened senses and observations, there's no way they'd miss it.

Heading out to the living area, I sit on the sofa and unbuckle my boots. We're going to be spending our time here for the next few days, so we might as well make ourselves at home. "Is there anything you two want to do or talk about?"

Don't say sex. Please, don't say sex. It's been a long day and my resolve is wearing thin.

"I wish to shower and retire to my quarters to regenerate," Link says. "Flash, you should do the same."

Flash doesn't argue, but it's clear he doesn't want to comply either.

Link doesn't wait for an answer. He strides off and disappears down the hallway.

I tilt my head into Flash's field of vision. "You don't have to obey him. You are your own person and can decide when you want to shower and go to bed."

Flash shrugs. "There's no sense in reminding Link that I am independent. He finds comfort in making the decisions for the three of us. He sounds autocratic and rude, but he means well."

"It's very obvious he's dedicated to your survival."

The *ding* of the elevator chimes and I haul my butt off the leather sofa and meet Tundra and Dune wheeling in a pallet of boxes.

"How's this for a delivery service?" Dune says. "If the whole warrior thing doesn't work out, we can start our own moving company. We'll call it Two Strong Guys with Wings."

Tundra rolls his eyes and ignores the comment. "We took the liberty of going back to Valorous Hall and asked one of the ladies to pack you up enough belongings for a few days. We also brought some staples and supplies."

I accept the two boxes marked with my name on them and smile as Flash scans the rest. "Thank you for this. I know it's late and we're all tired. This was very considerate."

"Not at all," Tundra says. "Do you need anything else? We don't have to leave. If you feel more comfortable, we are happy to stay and keep watch with you."

I wave off the big guy's concern. "No. You go. Take your mates home. We'll be fine."

"Are you sure?" Dune asks.

I nod. "I am. Thank you, though."

When Dune and Tundra leave, I carry my boxes to my room and check on Shift as I walk past. I hate to think he overdid it and harmed himself. He made his first attempt to use his healing powers count.

Mac is alive and out of danger.

I hope I can say the same thing about Shift.

"Are you well, Lady Lark?" Flash is standing at the door to the living room, watching me as I watch Shift.

"I'm worried about him," I explain, returning to the common area. "What he did to save Mac was both selfless and impressive. I'd hate for him to suffer because of it. I worry that me asking him to do it put his life in danger instead of Mac's."

Flash shrugs away my concerns looking more relaxed than I've ever seen him. He really is a devastatingly handsome man. "Try not to worry. Shift is regenerating. There is no indication of damage to his structural integrity or system functions. He simply drained his resources beyond recommended levels."

I draw a deep breath and exhale. "Good. I'm more than relieved. I'm hoping after a long sleep, he'll wake up and join us."

"He will. You'll see." Flash points at the other boxes on the pallet. "What did the Elbirfae warriors bring us?"

I chuckle at his enthusiasm. Flash is like a sweet puppy excited to have someone to play with. He's free of stasis and living his best life while taking in the wonders of a world he's been denied.

As a reader of thoughts, emotions, and memories, I can only imagine how much being awake allows him to experience so much from those around him.

Link is like the growly, guard dog overseeing his packmates. He doesn't trust us. Therefore, he doesn't want to say too much or engage.

If I'm reading him right, his reserve is partly to protect himself and his brothers from the disappointment of decommission and partly because he still feels defective.

Shift is a bit of both of his brothers. He has the hope for a new life but is more strategic than Flash. He wanted to help Mac because of his attachment to him and his desire to use his powers to heal but he also hopes that proving himself will solidify their place in our world.

It's strange, knowing what they are feeling and thinking. Lukas and Honor reminded me yet again that I don't truly know them, but when Link opened a channel for communication with me and told me I was their catalyst, their emotions and intentions began to leak through.

"Lady Lark?" Flash repeats. "May we look in the boxes?"

Right. "Sorry, I was daydreaming." I wave him away from the two boxes in the living room and point toward the kitchen. "Let's leave those until Shift and Link join us. You can help me with these."

Flash bounds over and peers into the box as I open things up. "What's in them?"

"Fresh food. Tundra and Dune brought us groceries. Tomorrow, I'll cook for us."

The smile he hits me with pulls all my strings. I'm trying to remain objective and be professional—I am—so why does it feel like these guys are breaking down every barrier I put up?

∽

Flash

Lark is incredible. Despite Link's doubts, I know she cares for us, and she is genuinely worried about our well-being. Having scanned her expression and her bio-readings as Shift over-exerted himself, there was no doubt how anxious she was to safeguard his health.

Before I think better of it, I lean forward and kiss her cheek. "No one has ever stood as our champion before. Thank you."

She eases back and swallows. "You're welcome."

The subtle tension she's held in her body all day grows more noticeable. She wets her lips, holding my gaze but remains frozen in place, her mouth slanting with indecision.

I offer her a regretful smile. "When we touched, I felt your fight to remain professional as our liaison, but I also felt the isolation you suffer from every day of your life. You don't have to be alone. I'm here. Let me be your champion."

A seductive spark lights in her bright green eyes and the sexual pull we share magnifies.

I draw my finger down the front of her shirt and brush the ample rounds of her breasts. "I promised you I wouldn't touch your skin without your permission, but it's becoming painful."

"Flash… it's been a long and emotional day."

"It has, and the emotion I've felt all day is desire. Somehow, you were meant for us. I can't explain how it happened, but it did. I feel it to the depth of my lungs and the core of my bones, and I don't believe I'm the only one who feels it."

I wait for her to make the decision but when more time passes and she doesn't, I step back. "Very well. Link was right. It's probably best if I wash and turn in for the night."

Lark catches my arm as I step away and pulls me back with an intensity that ignites a flare of heat through my systems.

"I don't want to be alone," she breathes against my lips, her body swaying toward mine. "You're not the only one who feels it."

Thank the stars. I wrap my arm around the small of her back and pull her tight against me. All the hard angles and edges of my body fit so deliciously into her generous curves.

Her mouth crashes urgently on mine and I kiss her back with equal fervor. I devour her thoroughly, hoping that if I cherish her completely, I'll stand out as the greatest kisser of any male who came before.

With a throaty moan, and without breaking our kiss, I lift her off her feet.

She splays her legs, wrapping them around my hips and I give myself over to the desire that has plagued me all day.

Carrying her over to the table, I prop her bottom on the solid surface. I make quick work of unbuttoning her leather pants and stripping them off her legs.

The moment I'm faced with all that smooth and creamy flesh, I suck in a breath. "You are incredibly beautiful."

My compliment makes her cheeks flush bright red. Does she not realize it? Has she not been told?

I will rectify that.

I look to see how to remove her top and faulter. With her wings there must be a way...

"I'll get my shirt. You take off your shoes so I can get your pants off."

"As you wish." I take off my shoes and am straightening as her top falls to the ground and I'm left with the glorious view of Lady Lark wearing only her underthings. "I have not lain with a female before, but I assure you that for intel gathering and assimilation into society, sexual excellence is part of our design."

Lark bursts out laughing. "Good to know. Thank you for telling me."

"How would you like me to ease you?"

She brushes a gentle hand against my cheek and smiles. "More of what we've already done will be wonderful. I'll let you know if I want anything different."

Excellent. I resume our kiss and tug her head back to expose her throat. My lips trail a scorching caress up the silky skin of her neck, and then I nip the smooth line of her jaw.

"Lay back," I say, my voice rough. Bending down over her, I press my mouth to her naval.

Lark gasps and her muscles clench and tighten beneath my kiss.

Face-to-face with the slip of silk keeping me from her core, I nuzzle forward and slide a hand against her calves. "Put your legs over my shoulders."

Her obedience warms me to my depths.

The snap of silk ends my restriction and I gaze down at her. "You're more beautiful than I imagined. You glisten." My voice cracks with emotion and I can't finish describing how much in awe I am of her.

"I ache, Flash. I need you."

Of course. "My apologies."

I grip her thighs, dip my head, and drag my tongue over the bud of nerves that hold her most intimate pleasures. Round and round, I flick and swipe.

When I touch her in just the right way, her body shudders and another rush of her essence warms my tongue. I growl, and the sound, calls another rush of cream to my mouth.

"Are you sure you haven't done this before?"

"Never. Although I believe keen interest might make me a natural." I slide my fingers up her ribs and underneath the band of fabric that binds her breasts. I find her nipple and give the hardened tip a little attention as I continue to dive face first, lapping at her folds, and probing her core with abandon. "You taste good. Oh, so good."

"Slecking hell," she gasps. "I'm close. Don't stop. Whatever you do, don't stop."

With my female on the edge of ecstasy, there's no way I'm stopping. Even if this bunker was under attack, the world would have to wait until after she finds her release.

With my hand still massaging her breast and tweaking her nipple, I tighten my hold, rubbing, pinching, and teasing the wildness building inside her.

Lark squirms, fighting the orgasm her body so desperately wants to realize. I nuzzle out of her entrance and focus on her clit. At the same time, I slide two fingers inside her and stroke her.

Her body's response is immediate.

Strong muscles contract within her, gripping and releasing, squeezing my fingers as she shatters. Crying out, her orgasm spills over in a glorious wave of cream against my mouth.

I still as her pleasure hits me in a searing sensation.

Her body's bliss sings through my nerves.

This is the most incredible use of my enhancements—feeling as her world falls away leaving nothing but ecstasy.

CHAPTER TWELVE

Lark

Flash chuckles, his mouth catching the feminine noises escaping me as his tongue challenges mine. "Again."

I hear the command and laugh. My core is still pulsing, throbbing with pleasure, gripping his fingers as I ride through the golden bliss of the aftermath.

"Again is a lovely idea, but it doesn't always work like that." If I wasn't still riding pangs of orgasm, I might be embarrassed at the thready pitch of my voice. "Besides, we've stepped beyond our boundaries. This isn't what we're supposed to be doing down here."

Flash draws his tongue from my core, up the center of my naked body, and circles my navel. "You are our catalyst. We are here to spend time with you, create a bond, and see how being near you enhances us further."

"Well, when you put it like that, I suppose we weren't as far out of bounds as I thought."

He looks at me and smiles, my release glistening on his lips. "I want you to come apart again. May I make that happen?"

I laugh. How's a girl supposed to say no to that? "You're very committed. I suppose if you have your heart set on pleasuring me…"

The triumphant smile he hits me with steals my breath. It's a good thing I'm flat on my back because there's no way my legs would hold me if I wasn't.

Gripping my thighs, he pulls me to the edge of the table and looks down, studying the globes of my ass. "I want to join with you. I need it. There is more to be experienced and I want it all."

He meets my gaze and waits, and I realize he's asking me. If I was anywhere near my right mind, I would stop this, but I'm not and I don't even care. Why shouldn't we? We're both consenting adults, I'm not fertile, and he's genetic perfection, so…

"Yes, Flash. I'd like that."

He pulls his hips back a bit, unties the drawstring of his pants, and presses the head of his cock against the moisture of my first release.

I groan and drop my head back. I spent two years living for everyone else. I need this.

I *deserve* this.

"Make me come again."

The growl that rumbles from his chest is carnal and calls another rush of moisture forward to slick his path. Gripping the edge of the table, I brace myself for the ride I feel coming. He pushes inside me, and my eyes roll back in my head. He's thick and ribbed and the invasion is possessive.

We both groan.

Genetic enhancements for the slecking win.

He stills for a moment to breathe, and I run my gaze down his smooth, muscled chest. "You feel good inside me. Way too good."

That spurs him into action, and he pulls out slowly before pushing deeper. The slide and glide are hot and wet.

When he stops this time, I'm gloriously full.

Almost too full.

"You're killing me with kindness here." I groan, wriggling on the table. "I need more. Faster. Harder."

"Yes, lovely. Anything you wish." Flash is an incredible listener and does exactly as I ask. He quickens his pace, his hands gripping my hips to pull me into each thrust.

The strength and power within him are incredible. I bet he could do this for hours. "Is this right?"

"Yes. That's so good."

A soft *click, click, click* sound has me opening my eyes and—slecking hell—Link is standing against the wall behind Flash. He's discarded his pants and is tossing off to the sight of Flash nailing me to the table.

His gaze locks with mine and my heart skips a beat. How can a scowl be so damned sexy. He's glaring at me like I'm his enemy and yet his body is saying something entirely different.

The voyeurism pushes me to the edge.

Damn, these men are beautifully made.

Watching Link's chest rise and fall with the breathlessness of his pleasure, while hearing Flash's breath escaping in heady bursts, and feeling the penetration as he fills me... it's unreal.

Flash buries deep, pumping his hips harder and faster. It's a frenzy of sensation. "I enjoy my cock coated with your heat."

I groan, lost in the bliss of being thoroughly taken, my ass squeaking against the surface of the polished table as he drives into me again and again. "Yes... I enjoy it too."

Link lets off a grunt and throws his head back, his muscles tense as his release hits. With his back against the wall, he sags, still pumping hard as cum streams from his cock and slicks his hand and muscled thigh.

He's got his eyes closed and a look of pure pleasure on his face.

It's too much.

The muscles in my core grab hold and I arch my hips, screaming as my orgasm hits. The pressure coiled deep inside me explodes and I'm shattered. It's intense and takes hold of me like nothing ever has.

My body comes apart and years of trying and fighting and having to be something for everyone else fall away.

Flash roars as his hips thrust forward and impale me. His beautifully golden skin glistens with sweat, his chest rises and falls in labored breaths. As throaty gasps escape, he arches back, and I watch him fall apart.

The super soldier created for emotional transference tells me everything without saying a word. I read his face, memorizing every emotion he's vulnerable enough to share with me: pleasure, torment, insecurity, terror.

When the waves of his orgasm fade, he releases his bruising hold on my thighs and collapses against me, breathless and panting.

Still buried inside me, he pulls me into his arms, and pads bare footed over to the couch. Chest-to-chest, and with me straddling his hips, I snuggle into his embrace.

I glance to where Link had been.

He's gone now and it's like I imagined the whole thing... but I didn't.

He might be the cold and broody one, but there's more to Link than anyone has learned yet.

Hitched breathing brings my attention back to Flash. He sucks in an unsteady breath and pinches his glassy eyes shut as he looks away.

I melt a little more. "Come here, sexy man." Holding him against me, I catch the view of us in the mirror. How the hell did we get here in one day?

"What's wrong with me?" he whispers, turning his head toward our reflections to look at me.

"Nothing's wrong with you. You've been through a lot and that was an intense moment shared."

"I'm sorry."

I ease back and cup his face between my palms. "Don't be. Not for a second. What happened between us was by far the most erotic, satisfying sexual encounter I have ever experienced. The fact that it stirred your emotions is a good thing. Don't apologize."

He swallows and tilts his head to the side. "Truth?"

"I swear. There's nothing wrong with emotions leaking out —especially when you're safe in the arms of someone who cares about you. You may have been engineered as a super soldier, but you are still a man, and you have feelings. Everything around you is new and overwhelming."

He chuckles. "I thought reading emotions was *my* genetic enhancement."

"It is. This is day one of your new life and there has been a lot of emotion to read. Give yourself a break. There's nothing to be sorry or ashamed about."

After another hug, I ease back and dry his cheeks with my thumbs. "Flash, what we shared was amazing. Thank you."

He grins. "I thought so too. And I feel my enhancements coming online stronger than ever. Your hypothesis about us spending time together strengthening our bond is working. My abilities are honing and becoming more focused."

I guess that makes it pleasure with a purpose... a scientific necessity. Ha. I'm not sure Honor and Lukas will buy that. "That's amazing."

"No. *You* are amazing." Flash leans forward to place a gentle kiss against my lips. "And very soon, I want to do that again and again."

I laugh. "You like that word. Something tells me I'm in more trouble than I thought."

Mac

I wake to the sound of a thousand hornets buzzing in my head and a cock so stiff I could punch a hole through a concrete wall if I ran into it.

What the hell happened?

I lift my hand to pull at the mask over my face and force my eyes to open. I fail the first time, the brilliance of overhead lights burning into my retina. "Feckin' hell, turn down the blasted lights."

"Got it. One sec, Mac."

Realizing I just swore at and ordered the Princess of Dornte, I curse. "My apologies, Princess."

"Don't apologize, Mac. I'm relieved you're alive to boss me around." She's back at my side a moment later. Leaning over me, she brushes a finger down my cheek. "I love that your Celtic heritage makes it so easy to make you blush."

"Yer a wicked woman, Princess."

She leans in and kisses my cheek. "I'm a relieved friend. Welcome back, Mac. You cut things too close on that one."

"He sure as fuck did," Lukas snaps, coming in to join us.

The princess might not have noticed what's going on under the blankets at my waist, but Lukas sure as fuck will.

I sit up a bit, bunching the blankets as much as I can over my hips. "How are the men?"

Lukas meets my gaze. "Dwa's family have been notified and will receive triple pay on the death benefit. Brody said he was under the truck when the bomb went off."

"Aye. He was ground zero, the poor lad. He never had a chance."

Lukas swallows. "We'll send him off as a hero, Mac, I promise you."

Good. That's good. "And the others?"

"Everyone else has recovered. Brody gave Tazz the phoenix tears as you intended, and that left you as the worst off."

"I hear the hostility in yer tone, but it doesna change a thing. I would do it that way again, and ye know it because ye wouldna do it any different yerself in the same situation."

Lukas props his fists on his hips and sighs. "Yeah, well, that's a truth easier taken from the position you were in. As a bystander, I don't like it one bit."

I chuckle and hold my hand out to clasp palms with my superior and friend. "What about the bodies? Have we identified them yet?"

"We have preliminary DNA and dental but without something to compare the readings against, that data is pretty much useless."

"What's yer best guess?"

"It's too early to say. We'll know more once we've finished with the search of the scene."

"When do ye think ye'll be able to get in there and look around?"

"We'll likely be able to poke around a little tomorrow, but it'll take a day or two before things cool off enough that we can look around with our equipment to get readings on things."

"Aye, well, I don't think I'll be makin' it to work today, boss. I'll take a couple of personal days on the horizontal, if ye don't mind."

"You got it, Mac. Take the whole fucking week if you need to."

"Och, no. I'm right as rain, ye'll see. Give me forty-eight hours and I'll be boots to blacktop."

"And thank the stars for that," Honor says. "This was too close, Mac. You've got to take better care."

"You got that right," Brody snaps.

My second in command is leaning with his shoulder on the frame of the door. "You lying piece of shit. You gave me those tears knowing full well you needed them more. *I'm right behind ye, lad,*" he says, making a damned fine impression of me. "Dune said you were flat out and circling the drain when he found you."

"All's well that ends well, lad. Let's keep our eyes on the horizon and put it behind us. Obviously, Dune got me back here in time to get some tears into me and it all worked out."

The three of them look at me and shake their heads.

"Wrong answer," Lukas says. "Try again."

I think about that for a moment. "What do ye mean? I was bad off. I can't imagine anythin' pullin' me from the brink other than Calli's magical miracle."

"It's not that we didn't try that," Honor says. "Yes, Dune got you here to us, and yes, we gave you phoenix tears, but you didn't respond to them."

The buzzing in my head is distracting, but I'm trying to keep up. "Then how am I here, lass?"

Lukas's brow arches. "Your man Shift put you back together. Lark brought him up and the guy went to work. Twenty minutes later he dropped to the floor unconscious, and your vitals stabilized."

"His enhancements aren't dormant?"

"Not anymore," Honor says.

"Were they lyin' or did we find their catalyst?"

Honor chuckles. "They swear Lark is their catalyst. Apparently, when they fought, Lark's blood got sprayed around and their traits began to activate."

"Do we believe that?"

Lukas shrugs. "We're holding off final judgement on that. So far, they've given us no reason to doubt them. For now, we'll accept what they're saying as truth. He did, after all, save your life."

I don't like owing those freaks a damned thing, let alone my life, but the honor of a soldier needs to be upheld. "Fine. I suppose I owe the healer a word of thanks."

Honor smiles and rests her hand against my wrist. "I'm sure that would be appreciated."

I breathe deep and let that settle. "This is goin' to sound awful, but which one is he?"

Lukas chuckles. "The one your cat bit into."

"Oh, aye, the one that was the color of fire. The others are closer to honey and flax."

Lukas nods. "Yeah, well, there's one more thing you might want to know about your fire boy and him saving your life."

"Yeah? And what's that?"

Honor takes my hand. "He says something in your saliva bonded the two of you when you bit him."

"What's that now? My head is still spinnin' but I think my record skipped there."

Lukas chuckles, fighting to hold back an amused smirk. "You heard right, Mac. He claims the two of you bonded and now you are *his* male."

"Fuck me."

CHAPTER THIRTEEN

Lark

I'm hoping the morning after the night before won't be as awkward as I worry. Link and Flash both showered last night and Shift is still sleeping, so that gives me a good chance to enjoy a shower and get ready before facing them both. I grab my clothes and toiletries kit and slip to the end of the hall unnoticed.

Seeing how these are barracks quarters, it's not surprising the bathroom is communal. There are individual toilet stalls, a wall of urinals, a line of sinks, and behind the wall of sinks, a large, tiled area with showerheads spread along the wall.

I set my clothes on the long bench opposite the showerheads and ensure the fabric is out of reach from the spray.

If I'd been asked to bathe in this kind of a setting a few years ago, I would've been anxious and mortified. Any modesty I had was lost during the two years I spent in a goblin concentration camp.

Privacy is impossible with a hundred people stuffed in a building, sleeping two to a cot or on any inch of the floor not covered by someone else. Nakedness, sex, vomiting, voiding wastes… it all becomes a rather public event.

I think about the few times I allowed myself to have sex in that setting. I was never comfortable having eyes and ears taking notice.

Last night… having Link stand there, gripping his cock and rocking himself to completion while watching us was a different experience entirely.

So slecking hot.

Knowing how close the three are and the link they share, I'm assuming Flash realizes Link was present for at least part of our sexual encounter.

Link is understandably possessive of his brothers. I don't want my affections to cause tension between them. I'm supposed to be helping them transition into modern life and assessing their intentions and allegiance toward the Crown of Dornte.

I clean up quickly, dress, and meet the two of them out in the kitchen.

Both men stand as I enter the room and I'm struck by the formality… or maybe that's my imagination. Maybe they were deep in conversation, and I startled them. That could easily be the case.

"Good morning, lovely." Flash's stride is direct as he closes the distance. His gait isn't as stilted and unsure as it was yesterday. With a graceful sway to his hips, he greets me, and brushes his lips over mine.

I swallow, breathing in his rich scent. He mentioned last night that for infiltration and intel gathering purposes, their designs included a mastery of sexual understanding.

He's proven that point.

My insides tighten and I give myself an inward shake. From the chiseled cut of his physique to the heat in his coy smile to the scent awakening my cells, I believe it.

I meet his affectionate gaze with a warm smile and step back to keep things from escalating.

Because boy do I want things to escalate.

Flash winks and smiles at where he's holding onto my wrist. Right. He can read me. That's not embarrassing at all. Well, if reading me makes him stand this tall, I'll deal with it.

It's like he grew twice as confident overnight.

The black cargo pants and tight t-shirt he claimed from the pile of clothes he found in his room set off the golden warmth of his skin to perfection.

"Good morning back. Did you sleep well?"

His expression shows no sign of the tension I suddenly feel through our connection, and I wonder if his emotional transference goes both ways.

He glances over at Link, and I can tell they're having one of their private conversations.

Link steps back and leans with his hips resting against the edge of the table. He's naked except for the gray pants Mac tossed him during our altercation yesterday.

Not that I'm complaining.

Link might be surly, but he's nice to look at.

Why are they acting weirdly? "What? It wasn't a trick question. Either you slept well, or you didn't."

When neither of them answers, I throw up my hands and start pulling out supplies for breakfast. "How are we supposed to build a relationship if you can't even answer a question as simple as that?"

"You're angry," Link says, his head tilting to one side as he assesses me.

"Not angry, no. Maybe a little frustrated. Yesterday we covered a lot of difficult ground, and I thought by the time we went to bed last night, we'd broken through some of the walls you put up."

"We did." Flash rounds the edge of the counter to join me. "Last night was wonderful."

When he holds out his hand, I give him mine. If reading me helps him to understand what I'm asking and why I'm frustrated, then I'll give him that.

After a moment he frowns. "We slept well. Our regeneration cycle is strangely disorienting outside of our cylinders, but we reached full restoration."

"Good. And yes, I imagine it would be disorienting being your first night of freedom." I choose some of the peppers and root vegetables from the fresh produce Tundra and Dune brought us last night and start chopping things for an egg casserole. "But you were comfortable? The mattress? The temperature? Your surroundings?"

Flash offers me a guarded smile. "We were physically comfortable, yes."

I hear the hesitation in his voice and stop to meet his gaze. "What? You're trying not to say something. Just say it, please. I don't appreciate word games."

Link pushes off the table and pads over to the other side of the island. "We slept well but were woken several times by your cries in the night. You made a point yesterday to say it was rude to bring attention to private instances which were involuntary and yet, when we tried to do as you asked, you still grow angry with us. We don't understand."

Well, shit. I set down the knife and draw a deep breath. "I'm sorry. You're right. This must all be so confusing for you, but the truth is, people are an exercise in contradictions. You did nothing wrong."

Flash exhales and tilts his head to meet my gaze. "Why was your sleep cycle interrupted by emotional outbursts? Is that a normal occurrence?"

I reclaim the knife and continue my preparations, distracting myself as I explain. "Two years ago, when the

Usurper Queen killed the royal couple and took over the throne, she had her minions slaughter the entire Amberloq army and then almost every Elbirfae in the quadrant."

"Why target the Elbirfae?" Link asks.

"Because up until that time, the Crown of Dornte had been guarded by the Elbirfae elite and without them, there was no resistance to her rule."

"It was a sound tactical decision," Link says, "though the genocide of a species is reprehensible."

I keep chopping. "Queen Laryssa ordered that a sampling of Elbirfae be captured and held captive: females, small children, and elderly and disabled males."

"And you were taken prisoner," Flash says.

I finish chopping the vegetables and set them aside. After grabbing the eggs and milk, I've tamed my emotions enough to continue. "I witnessed and experienced countless atrocities over the next twenty-eight months of confinement. At night, now that it's over, sometimes those horrors resurface in my nightmares."

Link frowns. "Can you not reprogram your regeneration loop to remove the unpleasant memories?"

Wouldn't that be nice? "Unfortunately, my sleep cycle doesn't work like yours. That is impossible."

"Does it happen every night?" Flash asks.

"I don't know. Sometimes I wake up if they're really bad and I thought that was all there was. I didn't realize I was crying out. I'm sorry I disturbed you."

"Don't be," Flash says, pressing a hand on my back. "There's no need to apologize when emotions leak out and you're surrounded by people who care about you, right?"

Having him repeat my words from last night sends a rush of warm tinglies through me. "That's very sweet, Flash. Well done."

He smiles at the praise and leans forward to kiss my temple. "I will think about it. Perhaps there is a way for me to minimize the emotions of those memories with my genetic enhancements."

Seriously, this guy melts me.

How could the scientists who designed them deem them defective? In just twenty-four hours they have grown so much.

Link scratches the back of his neck, his scowl deepening. "I will consider it as well. Interruptions to a sleep cycle are ill-advised. You are our catalyst. We will fix you."

I chuckle to myself, accepting the statement as it was intended and not how it sounded. "Thanks, Link. I appreciate your consideration."

~

Link

While Lady Lark and Flash converse in the kitchen, I look in on Shift and then return to my quarters. After being awoken from my regeneration cycle in the middle of the night, I took the chance to work more on gaining access to the data console by the elevator.

It took some ingenuity, but I was able to reroute some basic access functions to the desk interface in my quarters.

I close the door to the hallway and close my door as well. *Flash, I have work to do in private. Keep Lady Lark with you in the front.*

What work? Please don't do anything her people will consider egregious.

I promised you my discretion. Don't question my intentions again.

I cut off the neuro link and fight not to growl.

Flash has always been compliant and easy to deal with. In just twenty-four hours, I barely recognize him. Since our awakening, it's like he has a mind of his own.

I chastise myself. Of course, he has a mind of his own. I'm simply unaccustomed to him challenging me at every turn.

Part of me realizes how selfish that sounds, but the truth is, the three of us work well because there is not friction or contention. I discern the best course of action and we move forward as a united force.

My fingers skim over the touch screen of the desk interface, and I check on the things I've been working on. I've patched through to the camera systems and the exodus of Andras Brass and his scientists. At the time of their evacuation, he had two men down here working with him and six next generation soldiers.

Since they are no longer here, it stands to reason he's taken them to a secondary location. For what purpose? Are they designed to protect the Crown of Dornte and the Thornebane rule as we are, or do they have another objective?

The data and schematics on their design is deeply encrypted. My algorithm is working to unlock it, but it will take more time.

Perhaps Flash is correct, and I shouldn't filter through the systems without clearance. I don't care. We have the right to know about the models that were deemed better than us.

While that's sorting itself out, I check on the access pathways I'm even more interested in completing. The screen splits, giving me visual access to the stasis room where Alpha and Beta are still held in slumber.

"Not for much longer, my friends." I access their cognitive pathways and open a dialogue. "Trust me. You two shall be free soon enough."

Flash

Spending time alone with Lark is no hardship. She is warm, intelligent, fierce, and determined. She also has a talent for cooking. "This all smells so delicious."

She chuckles. "I think you're a little biased. Until now you've never experienced homemade meals."

"That might be true, but it doesn't make things smell any less enticing. I have access to over twelve hundred different smells and their combinations. I know what I'm talking about."

She laughs again and I let the sound fill me. No female should have to live through the things she did and yet, she not only survived, but she also thrived.

Lark became the caretaker for her people, she safeguarded them against the enemy who imprisoned her, and she became the warrior she needed to be to secure their future.

Touching her has given me incredible insight into her struggles but also into her desire to become a stronger warrior. "It's important to you that you gain the respect and recognition of the Elbirfae mates of the princess. Why?"

Her gaze narrows on me, but she doesn't seem angered by my question. "As I told you earlier, Laryssa, her witch, and her goblin army slaughtered almost all of my people. Dune and Tundra were away at the time and were spared. They represent the Snowy Peak and Desert Sand biomes. But my biome, the Forested Jungle, doesn't have any male warrior to represent it."

"Does the warrior representative have to be male?"

"Up until this point, yes."

I consider that and make the connections. "So, not only do your people need a worthy representative, but you are also the first female to assume that position. You want to both prove yourself and make your people proud."

She closes the door to the oven and warms me with a resplendent smile. "Exactly right. You understand perfectly."

"Then we will help you," I say, my conviction solidifying with every passing moment. "We will make you look good to your peers. We will train with you and make you a stronger warrior. And we will prove to your people that a strong, kind-hearted female is every bit the warrior representative as any male has ever been before."

Lark presses a hand to cup my cheek and shakes her head. "Where did you come from?"

I'm confused by the question. "Upstairs in the stasis lab. Remember? You found us there."

She bursts out laughing and pulls me into her embrace. "Yes, of course. I remember."

CHAPTER FOURTEEN

Lark

Link, Flash, and I spend the day getting comfortable with one another and then Princess Honor and her mates join us in the early evening. Dune and Tundra had contacted me several times over the course of the day assuring my safety and reinforcing their willingness to return at any time.

I assured them we were doing fine, and that I felt perfectly safe. Still, shortly after dinner, they messaged me they were upstairs checking on Mac and would come down to spend a few hours with us.

"But they won't decommission us," Flash says for the third time since I told them we'd be having guests.

"No. I promise you. They are visiting Mac in the med ward upstairs and wanted to spend time with you and get to know you."

"They didn't seem interested in getting to know us yesterday," Link snaps.

"Well, originally, there were questions about your allegiance and whether Valorous' initiative might've been corrupted in the two years since her death."

"It's a reasonable concern," Flash says.

"Yes. It is."

I'm not sure Link agrees.

Before anyone has a chance to say anything more, the *ding* of the elevator signals their arrival.

"Hello, hello," Princess Honor says, coming in with all four of her mates and a wolf cub.

Dune and Tundra have their arms full, and I laugh. "It's a good thing the elevator is as large as it is. You two keep bringing things down here."

Flash is at my side in a moment, and I can't tell if he's being protective of me, afraid of the wolf, or curious about what's in the boxes.

Maybe all three.

I go with the easiest one. "What did you bring us tonight?"

It's Lukas who dives in and starts opening the flaps. "We've got clothes, boots, some training weapons, blankets, fresh linens..."

"Baking," Dune adds.

"It's a mishmash, actually." Honor laughs, smiling at Flash. "Lark's been saying wonderful things about you boys today, so I wanted to sit with you for a bit. I was hoping we could talk about my aunt's program. I realize you were sequestered by the scientists, but any insights would be helpful."

Link is eyeing up Honor's fourth mate... the only one he hasn't met.

"My apologies," Honor says, catching the tension in his gaze. "Link and Flash, while you met Lukas, Dune, and Tundra yesterday, this is Shadow and our wolf cub, Moonshade."

Shadow is a striking dark elf with deep purple hair. He would attract attention even without his pupils being an almost iridescent white.

"Your eyes are very striking," Flash says, tilting his head to get a better view.

Honor smiles. "Shadow is a Fae Oracle. Do you know what that is?"

"Apologies, I do not."

"It's sort of like a prognosticator," Lukas says. "He has visions, and his extra-sensory sight took the place of his visual sight."

Flash takes a step closer. "And is Fae Oracle an unusual designation in the realm?"

Lukas nods. "It is."

"And what about the wolf? Is it friendly? May I touch its fur?" Flash asks.

"Moonshade is beyond friendly. She's a little too friendly for some. Go ahead. She won't mind."

Flash bends down to say hello and has his face thoroughly washed by the pup's tongue. The deep timbre of his laughter is infectious and soon all of us are chuckling... well, except Link.

Dune is still holding his box and tilts his head toward the back corridor to the sleeping quarters. "How about you boys show me where you're staying, and we'll get some of these clothes divvied up. Link, you could use a shirt, my man."

Link frowns down at his bare chest and then back at Dune. He doesn't argue, but he also doesn't look convinced.

"It's all right," I say, reading Flash's concern. "No one's here to decommission you. No stasis. No tricks. Dune just wants to sort through some clothes in your rooms."

He's not appeased.

"Dune, would you mind if Flash touches your skin? He can read thoughts and intentions through touch, and I've found it's the easiest way to get these boys to relax."

Dune juggles the weight of the box to one side and offers Flash his hand. "Fine by me."

After a moment of physical contact, Flash relaxes and then Link follows suit.

"Don't forget to set some things out for Shift," I call after them. "When he wakes up, I'm sure he'll enjoy having a few things of his own."

When Flash and Link take Dune and Tundra into the back corridor, I meet the curious gazes of Honor, Lukas, and Shadow. "We're still working on trust. From what they told me, they were brought out of stasis a few times, tested with one stimulant or another and then reinserted into their cylinders."

Honor shakes her head. "How do I make that right? I can't even imagine... well, I can, and that's what sickens me."

Shadow sets the squirming wolf cub onto the floor, and she takes off at top speed to look around.

Lukas gestures to the sofas and the four of us take a seat. "They seem to be coming into their own."

"They absolutely are. It's astounding how quickly they absorb and adapt."

Honor nods. "Yesterday, they seemed mechanical and awkward. Today, their voice patterns, gestures, and mannerisms all seem more natural."

"I understand the concept of super soldiers being adaptable to their surroundings, but it's an incredible thing to witness."

Honor presses her hand over my wrist. "And how are *you* adapting? It seems Flash has formed quite an attachment to you. Are you comfortable with that?"

I roll my eyes. "Honestly, I'm not sure what the hell is with this catalyst theory, but there is definitely a strong protective bond I feel for them. I'm not sure comfortable is the right word, but I also don't think there's much to be done about it. They are mine."

Lukas arches a brow. "Shift said the same thing about Mac. He said he needed to heal *his* male. Do you think it's them or you that's causing that bond?"

"I have no idea."

"May I ask a question?" Shadow shifts toward the front of the sofa cushion and turns to face me.

"Sure, go ahead."

"Does it matter from where the bond stems? You feel a protective bond with the three. They share that pull for you as their catalyst. Shift feels something similar toward Mac... Does it matter what's causing it or is the important part simply that it exists?"

I draw a deep breath and exhale. "I don't know."

Shadow smiles. "Perhaps your mind doesn't know because the facts are beyond your understanding. Perhaps the better question is what does your intuition know? What do you feel?"

Flash

I realize it's not charitable, but I'm not sorry to see Princess Honor and her mates leave. They were kind. They brought us new clothing of our own, so we don't have to wear the discarded articles left by the men who imprisoned us. They even brought us baking, which was delectable and addictive.

There is no good reason for me to hold ill feelings toward them and yet, I'm pleased when they leave.

Now, with Link off being Link and Shift still recovering from his healing, I have Lark's attention to myself once again.

Or at least I did until she fell asleep across my lap.

The two of us had been binge-watching FaeFlix shows for the past few hours and bit by bit she slumped to the side until I shifted her to lay down with her head in my lap.

I like this position a lot.

And no, not just because her mouth is so very close to my cock.

The truth is, other than a few moments when something suggestive happened in the program, I've been content to have her ebony hair fanned across my legs and her wings close enough to stroke.

"You're going to spoil me if you keep that up," she says, her voice more yawn than words.

"I thought you were sleeping."

"No. Just enjoying the moment."

A gentle caress along her bare arm tells me just how true that sentiment is. "You're more relaxed with me now than you were."

"Slipping into a coma will do that to a girl."

I hear the jest in her words, and I remind myself about sarcasm. She's not truly slipping into a coma.

She's teasing.

"What do you think? Do you like lounging in front of the television?" she asks.

"I like lounging with you. The fact that the television is on is nothing more than an excuse for me not to move for hours at a time."

When she doesn't reply I glance down at her closed eyes and smile. With another touch, I confirm my suspicions and find her mind falling deeper and deeper into slumber.

Lying my head back against the cushion of the couch, I close my eyes and follow her into her dream realm.

It strikes me that perhaps I shouldn't intrude without her consent, but then I remember how much she's encouraged me to self-advocate and make my own choices.

I'm not here as a spy gathering data. I'm here to explore my bond with her and learn more about my powers. And before this moment, I didn't even know I *could* follow her into her slumber.

I access my data record to save this moment forever: the scent of her in the air, the velvety softness of her feathers, the energy transfers I receive from touching her skin. It's incredible.

I am more at peace than I ever dreamed I could be in all my existence.

I sense when things shift, and Lark's dreams begin to grow dark. She feels a hopelessness she cannot let others see. They count on her, and she refuses to appear weak in front of them.

As her haunted mind takes over and her dream shifts to an endless loop of horror, violence, and fear, I navigate her emotions and replace them with bravery and a stalwart confidence that no matter what they do to her and the people around her, she will see them through, and everything will be all right in the end.

Her mind fights me, but her subconscious knows I'm right. She's safe now. Her people are safe. There's no need for her mind to keep dragging her into these emotions of defeat.

Lark, you win in the end, and everyone is well.

It takes a bit of effort to convince her, but eventually her dreaming mind releases the darkness and soars free once more.

That's it, my lovely. I have you and together nothing dark and dangerous can drag you away.

I smile as she lets off a feminine sigh and sinks deeper into a blissful slumber.

That's right. You are not alone in life any longer. You have me.

CHAPTER FIFTEEN

Mac

I wake in the wee hours and the world is one giant fuck-you fog of panic. Where the fuck am I? It hits me then. Right. Funny enough it's the buzzing of a thousand hornets in my head and the rod of steel throbbing between my legs that grounds me enough to remember what happened.

The explosion. The fire. Me nearly circling the drain fer the last time before Dune delivered me to Valorous' super soldier bunker.

Your man Shift put you back together. He claims the two of you bonded and now you are his male. Lukas' words bounce around in my brain and I try to rid myself of the horrifying sense that whatever he did to me will be permanent.

"Weel, no matter what I think about his contrived creation, I suppose if he hadn't been manufactured, I wouldn't be breathin'. I owe him that much."

Sitting up, I glance around the makeshift med lab they scrabbled together. Everyone seems to have taken off fer the night.

When Lukas and the others were here earlier, they said Lark was with the three down on sub-level five.

I check my watch and frown. It's really fuckin' late. Not that I'll be able to get anymore rest with this hive of bees bouncin' around in my head.

What the fuck did he do to me?

I sit up on the recovery bed and pull the line out of my arm. It's a struggle to get dressed, but after a fair bit of cursing and a few moments where I think I might faceplant, I'm decent.

Tazz is slouched between two plastic chairs in the hall, and I pat his arm and wake him up. "Take the bed, lad. I'm goin' down to five to stretch my legs and I've had enough time sleepin'. Get some proper rest. That's an order."

The guy is half asleep and doesn't argue.

I wait to make sure he gets to where he's going and once he hits the horizontal, I head to the elevator.

The shitshow shuffle isn't pretty and I won't be winning any land speed races, but it's a tortoise and the hare moment. I'll get there.

In the elevator, I pull the security pass still in my pants pocket and hit the button.

A headrush takes hold and the world becomes a spinning vortex that hits me all the way down to the empty pit of my stomach.

Okay, vertical might've been a mistake. I brace my palm against the wall of the elevator car and focus on pulling oxygen in and out.

Too soon, the elevator lets off a cheerful *ding* and then the doors whoosh open. My grand entrance will have to wait. I'm busy blacking the fuck out.

"Mac? Are you all right?"

Lark's voice comes from somewhere in the distance, but I can barely tell from which direction. It sounds like I'm trapped in a fishbowl and my hearing has gone wonky on me.

"Flash, help me get him to the couch."

Strong hands take over and my feet half drag and half shuffle across a gray, industrial carpet. When my ass hits a leather cushion, I'm eased back, and things begin to settle.

A cool cloth is set over my forehead and when I open my eyes, Lark's brilliant green gaze is taking me in. "What are you doing down here? You should be in bed upstairs being cared for."

"I'm great."

Her ebony brow arches, and she flashes me a knowing smile. "Yeah, I see that. You're right and tight and ready to take prisoners."

"Okay, so, I'm slightly less than great, but rumor has it, yer stayin' down here to keep an eye on our golden boys."

"Those rumors are true."

"Aye, then I'll be stayin' down here too."

She frowns. "Why?"

"Why not?"

"Because you were blown up and obviously still need time to heal. Wouldn't you be more comfortable back at Amberloq Hall? Or Thornebane Castle? Or recovering back in the Human Realm somewhere?"

I shake my head and regret the movement when the hornets get angry and buzz louder. "No lass. Ye see, when I woke up from what shoulda been my death, I was told a few things that don't sit well. I admit things are still fuzzy with all the buzzin' but I know enough about magic and my body to realize somethin' ain't right."

I tug the cloth off my forehead and focus on sitting up. "I need to speak to the healer. I don't feel right."

"That's understandable. You were hurt and need more time to rest."

"Aye, that's true but that's not what I'm talkin' about. Ye see, our boys here aren't the only ones feelin' the tinglin' of magic awakin' in their veins. That thing did somethin' to me, and I mean to figure out what it is."

"That *thing* did nothing but save your life." The room spins as I follow the voice and find Flax glaring at me with clenched fists.

Lark raises her hands and steps between us. "Easy, Link. This is hard for everyone, and Mac isn't well. Flash, help me get him to a room to lay down."

I swipe at the assistance and by the sheer force of my will, I stand under my own power.

Lark rolls her eyes and when the floor rushes toward my face, she grabs hold of my arm. Then it's all about the strong hands and the dragging shuffle once again.

One foot in front of the other, we make our way down a corridor of doors. Lark's muttering under her breath about stubborn, stupid males, and I have a strong feeling she's directing that at me.

"What did I do that fired ye up?"

"What did you do? I'm building trust and learning to communicate with these men, and you barged in, and then accused the selfless man that saved your life of messing with you."

My cat lets off a long, primal growl. "Somethin' is not right with me, lass. My cat is wild, my head is buzzin', and I've had a fuckin' cockstand since I arrived here yesterday."

She pauses in manhandling me down the hall and blinks "I'll file that little tidbit of 'Things I never needed to know' and try this again. You've been through a lot. You were nearly dead when Shift got to you. It's perfectly understandable if your body is reacting to the trauma. Maybe the magic you feel is residual from the healing."

"Aye, weel, if he'd show himself, I could find out."

She points at the bedroom door beside us and eases the door

open enough for me to see the man laying unconscious. "Shift healed you and he's yet to wake up. His system shut down and is still depleted."

The truth of that deflates a little of my ire and I exhale. "Somethin' isn't right, lass. I feel it in my bones."

"Maybe that's true, but coming down here and challenging them won't help. Trust me, Mac. When you feel like everyone is against you, judging your worth, and waiting for you to fail, a direct confrontation doesn't do anything but set you off."

I lift my hand to my head and wince. "Feckin' hell. I swear there's a swarm of angry bees bouncin' around in my skull. I can't think."

Lark gestures to the next room. "Lay down and I'll be right back. I've got something that will help."

I settle on the mattress and my instincts roar to the fore. "I want to keep my wits about me. It won't knock me out, will it?"

"No. It'll just work on your headache."

She goes across the hall, and when she returns, she's got a blue bottle of pills and a cup of cold water. She pours out two and I swallow them down without question. "Good. Now close your eyes. We'll see how you feel in a bit."

I don't want to be appeased, but I'm in no shape to argue. I check the time and curse. It's really fucking late. "All right, lass. We'll play it yer way fer now, but I'm tellin' ye, somethin ain't right."

Lark

After leaving Mac to lay down, I check on Shift, and then return to Link and Flash in the common room. It's a little unnerving to find the two of them in such a hostile state after the day we've shared in easy companionship. The tension in their expression is undeniable.

"Are you two all right?"

Flash is wearing a pained expression and sighs. "Mac knows Shift saved him and yet suspects him of something nefarious. I don't understand."

"And I don't appreciate the hostility he's spewing toward our brother," Link snaps, practically vibrating with fury.

Oh dear. "What Mac said was rude and wrong. No argument. Let's consider that he's not himself. He nearly died and isn't well yet. Try not to base your opinion of him on his worst moment."

Flash seems to take my advice to heart. "It was a terrible day. He was caught in an explosion and suffered catastrophic injuries."

"And as a commander, he carries the loss of life for one of his men. I don't know the man well, but I do know he cares about his team."

Link exhales. "I *can* understand that. If my brothers ceased to exist, the removal of their presence within our joint system would strike me as an acute loss. I would be angry as well."

Flash nods. "As would I."

They are so serious and odd in the way they interact, but they're not all that different from the rest of us. Even as bioengineered soldiers, they find comfort in creating connections with their brothers-in-arms.

"Why does your mouth turn up in amusement, Lady Lark?" Flash smiles, touching the corner of my smile with the tip of his finger.

"I'm grinning because even though your lives were difficult, you had one another. That must've given you some solace in those years."

Link glances at Flash and then he stares down the hall toward the private quarters. "I never considered it but you're right. We detested being trapped in a dark void, but we did have each other."

Those words hit me. "And you were always aware while you were in stasis?"

Link dips his chin. "Always."

"Why wouldn't Brass and his team ensure you were completely shut down?"

Flash fields that one. "A minimal level of activation was needed to ensure our systems didn't degrade in stasis. It was enough for our cognitive functions to be aware but not so much that we could wake up or move."

That's horrible. "How did you not go stir crazy? You were decommissioned for twelve years."

"We are aware," Link deadpans.

The magnitude of that blows my mind.

Link opens his mouth to say something else and then raises his gaze to the hallway behind me. "Ah, our brother wakes."

My heart skips in my chest to see Shift striding through the doorway upright and healthy.

I rush over and hug him before easing back and taking a good look at him. "How do you feel?"

"My systems are restored to optimal levels, but my nutritional reserves have been exhausted."

"I can help with that." I pull the baking dish from dinner out of the refrigerator and grab a plate from the cupboard. "Take a seat and I'll have you replenishing your needs in a couple of minutes."

"It's good to see you well, brother," Flash says behind me. "I couldn't feel you in our rest cycle and I worried."

He couldn't? Neither he nor Link mentioned that.

"Is that unusual?" I ask, sliding the plate into the microwave and setting the timer.

Link nods. "Very unusual. Before now we have always been connected through our stasis cylinders."

"What changed?"

"Either being freed from stasis or having our enhancements engaged, I expect."

Shift shrugs. "Whatever the reason, it was strangely peaceful to rest and recover alone in my own mind and body."

After hearing what the past twelve years have been like for them, I'm not surprised.

"Your feline male is here," Link says matter of factly, pointing down the hall toward the bedrooms. "He is angry and complains of buzzing in his mind and not operating at maximum capacity."

Shift frowns. "Perhaps I made an error during his healing. I do not recall completing it, actually."

"You wouldn't." I pull the plate of steaming food out of the microwave and grab cutlery. "You overexerted yourself and collapsed to the floor."

Shift tilts his head to the side and frowns. "Then perhaps the healing was incomplete, and my male suffers due to negligence on my part. I shall rectify that immediately."

When he turns to go back to the bedrooms, I raise a hand. "Shift, no. Not right now. Sit and eat. I gave him something for his headache. It will knock him out until morning at least."

"Then I should heal him while he sleeps."

"Maybe it would be best to wait until he wakes up and gives you permission. Until then, let's take care of your needs."

Shift doesn't seem to understand, but he doesn't argue. He climbs onto one of the stools at the breakfast bar and digs into the food on his plate. "My internal clock says I regenerated for thirty-one hours. Tell me what I missed."

Flash grins. "Lark and I had sex. She orgasmed two times and said it was by far, the most erotic, satisfying sexual encounter she had ever experienced."

Heat floods to my cheeks as their gazes lift.

"It was extremely arousing," Link says.

They each get that far away look that suggests they're talking mentally and then Shift smiles and nods. "I would like to have sex with you too, Lady Lark. I look forward to it."

Link nods. "What about now?"

My mouth falls open, but I've got nothing. "Uh... not tonight, boys. I'm going to turn in and will see you in the morning."

CHAPTER SIXTEEN

Link

The morning begins with my brothers and I spending time first helping Lark to prepare and then consume a meal. I admit, the difference between a freshly cooked meal and the warmed contents of military rations is extreme. I never realized food could be so satisfying.

"And that got me thinking about Alpha and Beta sitting there in stasis," Lark says, washing a plate and then handing it to Flash to dry. "Do you think they are aware too?"

Shift pours himself more juice. "They most certainly are. At least as aware as we were."

Lark frowns. "That's not right. I'm going to talk to Princess Honor and her mates about that today. It's barbaric to put you through something like that. I didn't like the idea of stasis when I thought you were unaware, but if their minds are processing the passage of time and even the smallest bit of your surroundings, we can't let that happen."

I agree. That's why I initiated their waking sequence yesterday.

You did what? Flash fumbles the plate in his hand, and it goes clattering across the counter.

Be calm, brother. You're over-reacting.

Lark collects the plate as it skates past her and examines it. "Not broken. No worries. Just be careful. Wet plates can be slippery."

"I'm sorry, lovely. I got distracted for a moment." Lark pays him no more attention and when she continues with washing up, he turns his focus back to me. *You promised you wouldn't do anything to upset them and question their trust in us.*

And I kept that promise. I programmed the system to bring them out of stasis on a regular maintenance cycle. With Brass and his team gone, no one will know any different.

You underestimate them, brother.

No. You overestimate them.

Flash looks to Shift for support, but he merely holds up his hands. *I was unconscious for a day and a half. I'm still catching up.*

Lark finishes with the dishes and dries the counter. "I'm going to organize a few things in my room and then have a shower. Are you boys all right?"

"Of course," Flash says.

The three of us watch her retreat and I wait until the latch of the door to the bedrooms clicks into place and we have the common area to ourselves.

Shift projects his thoughts toward me and points down the hall. *Lady Lark is lovely and has been kind to us. I don't want to lose her trust. Feeling how strong Flash's enhancements are engaging, I believe it is Lark's influence. I don't want your actions to ruin that for us.*

Thank you, Flash snaps.

And I agree. I read the skepticism in Flash's gaze and hold up my hands. *I agree she is lovely and spending time with her is a boon. I simply don't trust her convictions to allow us a life without threat of being decommissioned.*

She volunteered to remain here with us and acclimate us to life in the realm, Flash says.

And if we fail to meet her expectations what happens?

The same thing that happens every time they've allowed us to wake, Shift says. *They'll list our deficiencies and put us back into stasis.*

She isn't like them, Flash insists. *She wants us to be successful. I feel it when I touch her.*

And why is that? I ask. *After all these years, why would she have any investment in our success or failure?*

Shift sets his glass onto the table. *We were created to be tools in battle. She is trying to prove her place in the hierarchy of warriors. Perhaps she believes that taking us on as a side mission might earn her credibility with her peers and in front of her superiors.*

Agreed. It is the most logical explanation. And that is why I believe we should use that to our advantage.

Shift glances over to me. *How so, brother?*

If it is her desire to become a fierce warrior, perhaps we help train her.

Shift nods. *We could gain her trust and see what happens. If all goes well, we live our lives, but if something happens and we are to be decommissioned, we could leave this place.*

Flash shakes his head. *And go where?*

I've been thinking about that, I say. *If what she says is true and the realms are united, we could flee to the human realm and live in peace.* I replay the hand-to-hand confrontation we had when we first met. *She needs a great deal of training. When she fought, she relied exclusively on force and determination. Her skill is minimal.*

Then we offer to train her and build on our rapport. Shift says.

Flash can gauge her feelings toward us, If there's any inclination she intends to recommend putting us back in stasis, we leave at once.

Can we leave? Shift asks. *What about our directives to serve? They are programmed directly into our core.*

Leave that to me. They have yet to realize the extent with which we can interface with the building systems and the backup server. *I will study our coding and find a way to free us from compliance.*

Flash looks displeased. *What if they find out and take your actions as a sign we can't be trusted? What if us seeking a break in their control causes them to judge us dangerous or untrustworthy?*

Then I will be careful not to let them find out. You can help with that. You can keep her busy and ensure she doesn't come forward to this part of the floor.

I don't like it. I think earning the trust of Lady Lark and Shift's human is the better course.

I glance at the closed door. *Duly noted. For now, we'll play their games and seek their approval. Only when and if it becomes necessary for us to leave will we entertain the idea of defecting.*

Flash makes no attempt to hide his frustration from us on the link, but it's not his fault. His genetic conditioning makes him much more predisposed to emotion than Shift or me.

Still, there's no concern about his allegiance or him not following through with us.

I reach out and brush his mind with as much understanding as I can send him. *No matter what happens, I will take care of us. We are brothers.*

Flash nods and heads for the door to the bedroom quarters. *Yes. Brothers.*

~

Flash

Despite what Link says, I don't believe Lady Lark will judge us and put us back in stasis. Link is cynical and lacks faith in anyone other than the three of us. That's fine for him but he's incorrect.

In many things, Link knows best.

When examining the intentions of people, my knowledge is better.

I enter the bathing area and move to examine myself in the mirror. The few times the scientists woke us to try to stimulate our enhancements, they kept our hips swathed in fabric bands and fed us from cellophane bags.

Lark doesn't realize what it means to us to be given clothes and fresh food… and sex. She has done more to make us feel accepted and alive in two days than anyone else did in any of the times we were awake before.

Water sprays behind the wall I'm facing, and the hiss sparks my imagination. Lark is there, water running down the gentle curves of her body and dripping off those glorious ebony wings.

"Is someone there?" she asks, her voice echoing a little against the hard surfaces.

"It's me, Lady Lark."

She chuckles softly. "Just Lark, sexy man. After last night, we can both agree that while I am female, I'm no lady."

I fail to understand that.

The water shuts off and she steps around the end of the wall of sinks and winks at me. Her hair hangs long and dark against her bare shoulders and she has a towel wrapped under her arms. It hides her body from the center of her chest to the top of her thighs.

I swallow and face her, setting my hands on her hips. "You look delicious. Shall we have sex again? I put it at the top of my favorites list."

She laughs. "I'm sure that's true, but I'm supposed to be here as an observer. What happened last night—while amazing— wasn't a good choice. Like you, there are people watching me and waiting for me to fail. I need to prove to them that I'm a good soldier and getting caught in a sexual act with the three men I'm supposed to be observing isn't likely to impress them."

I wave that away. "Our sexual connection opened my emotional enhancements. You helped me."

She pads, bare-footed, around me to face a mirror and pulls a brush through her hair. "I'm glad it helped you. In truth, it helped me too. It's been years since I surrendered myself to passion. Everything in my life the past few years has been incredibly guarded."

"That sounds exhausting."

"It was, actually." She finishes with her brush and takes a second towel to squeeze the water out of the length of her hair. "So, our encounter was mutually beneficial. It's one of the reasons I refuse to regret it."

"Should I regret it? I don't. Not even a little bit."

"No. I'm not saying that. You are allowed to feel however you feel and that's perfectly all right."

"Good, because sex is my favorite."

She sets her hand on my shoulder. "How about we try not to announce that quite so often. If someone asks you, I don't want you to lie, but sex is a private thing and I'd prefer it to remain our secret, if you don't mind."

"Because you're a private person," I say.

"That's right." She sets her brush back into a small blue bag with a zipper up the center and pulls out a small tool with synthetic bristles on it. After trailing a line of bright blue gel on the bristles, she runs it under the water and then puts it in her mouth.

I watch in fascination as she flicks and brushes and moves the tool around. "Is what you're doing supposed to feel sexual because it's making me hard watching you push and pull that tool in your mouth."

Lark spits blue foam into the sink laughing. "You've really got a one-track mind, don't you?"

"What does that mean?"

"It means you're focused on sex right now."

"It's a new experience. I'm still processing it."

She dries her mouth and pegs me with a look. "Eating a home-cooked cheeseburger with fried onions was also a new experience, but you're not fixated on that."

Now it's my turn to laugh. "But the cheeseburger didn't make me orgasm and feel like my body might explode with pleasure. Almost... but not quite."

She laughs again, leans forward to kiss my cheek, and then collects her little bag of things. Pulling out a package of more mouth tools, she hands me one. "It's called brushing your teeth. When we wake up, after we eat a meal, and before we go to bed, we brush our teeth and clean our mouths. It's not sexual."

She hands me the tube of blue gel and smiles. "A little dab, a splash of water to make it froth, and then clean your mouth."

When she leaves me staring at the set up, I figure I might as well give it a try.

That's what life with our catalyst is about, isn't it? Our enhancements growing stronger and unlocking new experiences.

Still, I have a feeling this won't be as good as sex.

CHAPTER SEVENTEEN

Lark

I dress for the day and try to push their comments about sex out of my mind. It is perfectly natural that Link found watching us arousing and that Flash wants to repeat the experience.

Hell, *I* want to repeat the experience, but my reasoning is sound. I'm not here to get laid by three gloriously chiseled specimens of perfection.

However appealing that idea might be.

I'm here to learn about them, help them develop their enhancements, and determine their commitment to the Crown of Dornte versus any of the other players who might've corrupted their core directives in the two years since Valorous was killed.

While I wait for the boys to get dressed and ready, I decide to venture into the exercise room to work my way through a couple of circuits of push-ups, sit-ups, and lunges.

When my muscles sigh with a triumphant soreness, I shift

my focus toward a few of the combat sequences I learned in the prison camp.

Prior to being rounded up and forced into that goblin camp, I'd never considered being a warrior. I had my sights set on working with the biome council to serve my people and my community.

It seems the universe had other plans for me.

I check my stance in the mirror wall and bring my elbow closer to my ribs. Swinging my wing around in a sharp crack, I step into my punch.

Being a Biome General and representing the Forested Jungle is still serving my people.

It's just a much steeper hill to climb to get good.

I'm finishing the final rep of a set of jab-cross-hook combinations when the boys come in and join me. They're dressed to workout too and I lock down all my throbbing female reactions.

Drool is bad for the workout mats—it makes things slippery.

"May we join you, lovely?" Flash's nickname is a little personal for mixed company, but I like it better than the formality of Lady Lark.

And who are we kidding, the three of them share everything including thoughts and emotions. Having sex with Flash is the same as having sex with all three.

Only not.

Shift bows his head and peels off his shirt, exposing a glorious eight-pack and that seductive V that men get from their hips down to their cocks. "My brothers and I were wondering how to repay the kindness of you volunteering to stay with us, so we don't get put back in stasis."

I wave my hand between us and shake my head. "Don't be silly. You have nothing to repay. I don't want you put back into stasis."

"Why?" Link says.

I glance over to him and stretch my shoulder out by pulling

it across my body and securing the back of my arm. "Honestly, it's a bit of a jumble. When we first learned about the possibility of super soldiers, I imagined the results of this experiment would be violent automatons geared for war. The three of you showed me how narrow minded that opinion was."

"You weren't completely wrong." Flash sets down one of the boxes Lukas brought last night and starts pulling out practice swords. "Our first contact was the three of us attacking you."

Yes, it was.

Link moved to subdue me, Flash and Shift took on Mac, and all hell broke loose. They overpowered us, Mac transformed, and then his cat lunged from the floor and turned the tides.

Shift rubs at his clavicle, and I wonder if he's remembering Mac's canines puncturing his flesh.

Why does that feel so erotic?

Damn, now Flash has got me keyed up with sex on the brain. "It's true, you threw the first punches, but something happened to me as well. You boys say I am your catalyst, but I think that connection somehow goes both ways."

"Explain." Link's gaze narrows.

I hear the mistrust lacing his tone but choose not to take offence. "I'm not sure I can explain. It's completely inappropriate and nothing I intended, but I find myself disarmed by you three."

Flash frowns. "You have never poised a weapon and we have never taken it from you."

"Not physically disarmed, sweetie. I mean... I'm here in a professional capacity and intended to keep myself distant and objective. But when I'm alone with you three... I feel a pull for something completely different."

"What kind of pull?" Link steps closer, his body languid and powerful.

Watching him in the throes of release while Flash and I were giving in to the carnal pleasures of this bond I feel...

Shit, I'm doing it again.

The three of them are inhaling deeply and I have no doubt they're sensing my arousal. I draw a steadying breath and push down the warm flutter in the center of my chest.

"I feel a pull too," Shift says, prowling forward like a graceful predator. "It's desperate and hungry. It burns in my loins, and it is focused on both you and my feline male. I felt it before I healed him but since forming that connection to save his life, it has grown much more powerful. I want things... Dark, seductive things."

Slecking hell.

"Is the pull you feel like that?" Flash asks, brushing a hand against the undeniable bulge pressing at the front of his workout pants.

I swallow, my underwear now completely soaked through. The way these three overshare is refreshing but at the same time, it's a lot to take in. "Well, yes. It's completely out of character for me to give in to sexual impulses like I have. I'm usually a driven, focused leader, but something about you knocks me off my normal stride."

Flash grins at me. "If you need to investigate that more, I am willing to help with the experiment."

I laugh and hold up my finger to keep him at a distance. "I'll keep that in mind. But other than the mind-blowing, totally inappropriate sex, my instincts make me want to protect your interests and ensure your well-being. That makes no sense to me. I'm not one to get emotionally invested in others and that's not why I'm here."

Link may not have included me in his mental communication channel but the longer I'm with them, the more his emotions leak through.

He doesn't believe me.

That's fine. I'm here for the long game.

I point to the wooden swords Flash has unpacked. "What have you got in mind?"

Shift straightens. "Oh, that's back to the point of my earlier comment. We thought we might repay you for your kindness by working with you on your combat skills."

Link's gaze is locked on mine. "I mentioned yesterday, you have strong instincts and determination but need training to hone your fighting efficiency."

"I remember." The criticism stings, but I force a smile. "That's generous of you to offer, but not necessary. I'm here to help you acclimate. You owe me nothing in return."

"We insist," Shift presses. "The three of us need to exert physical energy as well. We can teach you some higher-level points which will improve your abilities."

"All right. I'll give you a moment to warm up and stretch and then we're on."

～

Mac

I'm not sure what Lark gave me, but the bitch lied to my face. She had to know those pills would knock me on my ass and she swore they wouldn't.

Trust is a delicate thing, and she hadn't earned it.

Now, she never will.

She exposed both of us to the threat of those three machines and my life wasn't hers to risk.

Rolling to my feet, I'm halfway to the door when the head-rush hits and the world spins. I growl, toppling into the hallway and straight into the clutches of Flame—the one I bit.

"My male. Are you malfunctioning?"

The jackass moves to sweep my legs out from underneath

me to lift me and cradle me against his chest. My cat lets off a long, snarling hiss. "Don't even think about it."

Flame reconsiders the white knight gallantry and helps me to sit on the floor before I fall on my ass.

Good enough.

I slide down the wall and rest flat on my back as the world spins back into focus.

"Apologies. If my healing has inadvertently harmed you, I will make it right. My sole intention was to restore your health and save your life."

I close my eyes and my stomach whirls, so I cut that shit off and open things up again. "I accept yer apology, but I dinna think me feelin' faint is yer fault. I haven't eaten in two days and with the amount of blood they tell me I lost, my body's been through the wringer. I got up too fast, is all. This is on me."

The golden-skinned male lays down on the floor beside me and looks up at the ceiling. "And does laying here make you feel better than me carrying you to my bed?"

"Aye, it does."

"Why? The floor is hard, cold tile and the lighting is harsh and offensive to my eyes."

I try again to close my eyes and things go much better this time around. "It's not the destination that was the problem. I'm a warrior and I'll not have ye carryin' me like a child even if I was knockin' on death's door."

He shifts beside me. "Is there a door to death?"

"It's a figure of speech."

I draw a couple of deep breaths, filling my lungs to clear my head. The scent of him sets my cat on the prowl again. He smells like... I'm not even sure what.

It's sweet... maybe minty? And there's something else. My growl is nothing I can hold back. He's aroused. He's lying here next to me and he's fucking aroused.

What's even worse… my body stiffens and my cock takes that moment to weigh in. My body wants what he's offering, but that's insane.

"Are you well, warrior?"

"I shall do."

"Lady Lark said you complained about insects in your head last night. I assure you, I had no part in that. There were no insects involved in my healing."

I chuckle even while finding none of this funny. "Weel, it wasna really insects I was complainin' about but only the sound of them buzzin' in my skull."

"And do they still buzz?"

"Not nearly as badly no. It seems yer Lady Lark was correct, and I did, indeed, need more rest."

"So, you do not suffer?"

My blood is hot with need and my cat wants to roll this guy over and fuck him hard from behind, but that's not the kind of suffering he means. "Once I get some food in my belly, I'll be fine."

"We have food. Lady Lark made first meal before she and my brothers went to the training room."

"Did she now? Lady Lark has been a regular happy home-maker with the three of ye, hasn't she?"

He doesn't respond to that, but it was rhetorical anyway. I don't give a shit how she treats them. To me, they are not to be trusted until we've had a chance to comb through every bit of their programming.

"Mac? Shit. Are you okay?" There's a shuffle of boots racing down the hall and then Lukas is standing over me. "Fuck, you're white as a ghost."

"Aye. I got up with a little too much oomph and thought a time-out here where it's cool would be good before I take another run at it."

"Shift? Is he all right?"

"He said he's more comfortable here than me carrying him to my bed."

I crack an eye open and catch Lukas's amusement. "Not a word, asshole. It's not like that and ye know it. But he speaks the truth, I told him to let me be rather than carry me to the closest bed. What I need now is to eat. I've got nothin' in me."

"I can help you there. I brought you one of Hawk's special French roasts with two creams, and Shadow sent a breakfast casserole and biscuits for the bunker buddies."

"Bless ye both." I hold up my hand. "How about a little help fer an old friend."

"You got it."

Lukas clasps hands with me and hauls me to my feet. After giving me a moment for my head to settle, he helps me to the living room and sits my ass on the back bench of the table. "Here, sip your coffee and I'll grab you a plate and get you started."

"Yer so damned domesticated."

Lukas laughs. "A group marriage will do that to a man. With five of us in one living space, we all have to do our part or things start to get unevenly weighted."

He sets a plate in front of me, and I go for the biscuits first. "Fuck, they're still warm."

Lukas grins. "Only the best for Alpha-1."

I break the biscuit in half and pop it into my mouth, groaning as the flavors warm my tongue. "If ye weren't married to four other people, I might kiss ye fer this."

Lukas laughs. "Such a tease. In all those years when we were single you never once made a play."

"I guess I like the unattainable."

Lukas is about to respond when he realizes we're being observed. "Sorry, Shift. We get clowning around and sometimes forget there are others in the room. So, how are you feeling now that you're finally regenerated after the healing?"

"I am well and operating at maximum efficiency."

Lukas grins. "I'm glad to hear it. And where are Lark and your brothers?"

"We are training her in combat. She feels judged based on her lack of combat skills and we owe her a debt. Lady Lark offered us tits for tats."

I choke and almost spit biscuit at my commander. "I think ye mean tit for tat, my man."

The male tilts his head and looks at me, his warm, caramel eyes confused. "Is that not what I said?"

"Almost," Lukas says, chuckling. "Tits are a slang term for a lady's breasts and tats is the shortform for tattoos." He rolls up his sleeve to show me an inked design in his skin. "Tit for tat is a saying on its own. It means I help you and you help me."

I nod. "Then that is what I meant. She helped us unlock our genetic enhancements and we wish to help her unlock her potential to be a great warrior."

"Tit fer tat," I repeat nodding. "Aye, that's decent of ye. So, ye really believe Lark was the catalyst to unlock yer powers?"

"Not just her, but something in the enzymes of her blood."

"So, during the battle, you were exposed to her blood and things started to change immediately?" Lukas asks. "Lark mentioned when she ordered you to stand down, that's what stopped the fight."

"For Link, that is true."

I chew the casserole and wash it down with coffee bliss. "But it wasn't the same fer all of ye?"

"No. Link was affected by her blood during the altercation of first contact. Flash and I tasted her blood during the time spent in the interrogation room. That's when we felt our enhancements begin to unlock but they didn't truly take hold until later."

"So, what stopped ye in the battle then?" I ask.

Lukas sits back and crosses his arms, a smug smirk lifting his cheeks as if he knows what's coming.

"What's the look?"

"Wait for it," he says. "Go ahead, Shift. What brought you up short during the battle?"

The guy turns those stunning eyes on me and smiles. "It was our bond."

I blink. "Wait. What's that now?"

"The bite your feline beast inflicted sent a rush of awareness through me and woke something. Your beast claimed me, and I submitted to him. We are bonded—you and I."

I sit there and let that little ray of sunshine filter through the gray matter of my mind.

"Bonded ye say."

He dips his chin. "Yes, you are my male. I feel a pull to serve you, to be near you, to please you. I don't know what it means, but I know it means something."

I swallow but have no idea what to say about that. "That's flatterin', lad, but maybe ye got yer wires crossed. It's been a busy two days. Let's not read too much into anythin' just yet. In fact, would ye mind goin' to check on yer brothers and Lark workin' out. I'd like a private word with my commander and then we'll meet back up with ye in a bit."

The male searches my gaze. "Have I angered you?"

"Och, no. Why would ye think that?"

"The micro expressions around your eyes, the tension in your voice, and the increase in your heart rate are all indicators of emotional upset. Should I not have said anything about you being my male?"

Feckin hell. "Yer fine. If ye would. I really need to speak to Lukas privately."

The guy dips his chin and pushes off toward the common area of the floor. When the guy is good and gone, I unlock my muscles and meet Lukas's gaze. "What the fuck was that about?"

Lukas busts up laughing and shakes his head. "I have no idea but when he saw Brody and I working on you upstairs, he strode straight over like he might rip me to pieces and said he needed to heal his male."

"Ye don't need to enjoy this so freely, fuck ye very much."

Lukas rubs his eyes and tries to sober. "Sorry man. After witnessing Hawk get bonded to Calli, and then Keyla and Creed, and then feeling the pull I had with Honor... there's no way I'm discounting this as a possibility. Let me ask you this. How's your sex drive?"

I glance down at the throbbing bulge in my pants and curse. "Fuck me. Do ye think me wavin' a steel rod around has somethin' to do with him?"

Before Lukas can answer, a spearing pain jabs into my skull and the buzz of hornets return. "Feckin' hell. Did I have a head injury from that explosion?"

Lukas shakes his head. "No, but Creed and Keyla had a buzzing in their head before they accepted their mating. They said it was a beacon leading them to their destiny together."

I raise a hand to my forehead and curse. "Yer startin' to piss me off with that shit. I'm not bonded to a genetically conjured soldier. I'm not! So, stop sayin' that and give me somethin' to ease this feckin' headache before my brains leak out my ears."

Lukas pulls a cigarette case out of a pocket of his pants and waggles his brow. "I've got some of Hawk's special stash. We'll tend to your headache quickly and then round up the three and get to business."

"Yer takin' them out?"

Lukas nods. "Alpha Squad cleared the debris from the barn and found the escape passage. We know where the little weasels went, but it's locked behind a biometric scanner, and we've had no luck cracking the coding of how to get it open."

My cat lets off a long growl. "Whoever was behind that detonation is mine. I'm gonna rip those fuckers' throats out and throw their carcasses to the wolves."

Lukas hands me a hand-rolled cigarette and flips open his lighter. "And I'll be right there to cheer you on. Now, let's tend to that headache of yours."

CHAPTER EIGHTEEN

Flash

"You're telegraphing your intentions, Lady Lark," I say, jumping to my feet to join her and Link on the training mats. "Anyone with advanced training will see your attacks coming before you even get the chance to strike.

Moving to stand behind her, I set my hands on the fabric of her hips and position her properly.

"And remember, don't be too anxious to start the fight. You can learn a lot about your opponent by studying the way they move and set up before engaging. Everything tells you something: the tension in their frame, the way they distribute their weight, whether they have a dominant side or not..."

"Flash is correct," Link says, his hands up and at the ready. "It all means something. Now, if I come at you like this, how do you counter?"

He takes a slow, advancing step with his forward leg and brings his hand around and in line as if he's about to punch her.

She takes the half step back the way we showed her, brings

her wing up to block the strike, and while she's pushing that arm out of the way, she steps inside his reach and simulates a strike to his ribs.

"Exactly, right," I say, excited to see how quickly she picks things up. "And now that you're inside his defenses?"

She moves to sweep his foot but instead of being fast and direct, the swinging arc of her leg allows her opponent—in this case, Link—to step back, make her overstep, and sweep her leg instead.

Lark lands on the mats on her lovely backside and grunts. "Slecking hell."

"It's fine." I rush over to help pull her up. "We've only just begun to train you and you've already improved. You said we had days before Princess Honor and her mates will weigh in on our status here. That's plenty of time."

She laughs and offers me her hand to help pick her up. It warms me how freely she allows me to touch her now. She's trying to gain our trust, but in the process, I have gained hers as well.

Shift joins us. He looks unsettled, so I reach out across the group link the three of us share. *Are you well, brother? Has something happened to your male?*

My male is awake and speaking privately with his commanding officer.

Why do you look so unsettled?

I told him about the tingling of his bite and my submission, and he said nothing in return. Perhaps I am defective and there was no enzyme bond with him as I believe.

Then why would you stand down in the fight? Link asks.

I don't know.

No, brother. There is something between you two. We feel it through your link. Also, you would not abandon a directive for no reason.

I agree. *Perhaps your male simply doesn't feel the bond the same way you do.*

Shift nods. *That's possible. Perhaps the discomforts he mentioned have nothing to do with his injuries or my healing. Perhaps his bond has hit him differently than mine.*

"Hey, guys?" Lark says, waving a hand into our line of sight. "I get that you have your own stuff going on, but when the three of you stop interacting with the world and just stand there and stare at one another, it's unnerving."

"Apologies, Lady Lark," Shift says, dipping his chin to show his respect. "I am trying to navigate a situation I am ill-prepared for. My brothers were simply trying to help me."

"Please, no more Lady Lark. Just Lark is fine."

"As you wish."

"And, in future, if you don't want everyone to know you can speak telepathically, maybe you should work on being more discrete."

"You are aware of our conversations?" Link asks.

"That you're having them? Yeah. I know what your enhancements are, and when you talk like that you zone out and it's obvious."

"Will it be bad for us if people know?" Link asks.

"That's for you to decide. All I'm saying is you're telegraphing a gift that might be more beneficial to you if other people don't know you're using it."

Link nods. "A wise observation."

Lark is about to say something more when Lukas leans in the doorway. "Good morning, folks. I need you to clean up and dress for a mission outside the bunker. I'm taking Mac with me now to go over the logistics and we'll meet you up top."

As quickly as he arrives, he leaves.

I look at my brothers and they are as concerned as I am. "We've never been outside. Why would they want us to go outside?"

Lark shrugs. "I don't know. I guess we'll find out when we get up there."

"What's really going on?" Link asks, striding toward her.

She holds up a hand to stop him and glares. "I don't know. I haven't been briefed on anything. You were standing right here when Lukas told all of us together."

Link looks to me and I understand immediately. Without asking for permission, I take her hand.

The connection of skin to skin brings me a rush of emotion: anger at my impulse, sadness we didn't trust her, and searing regret that she let her guard down and befriended us.

Her right cross cracks into my jaw and sends my head around on a swivel. The force is shocking and knocks me back onto the mats. "How dare you?"

I roll with the momentum and get back onto my feet. "Apologies, lovely—"

"—No! Don't call me that. I am Lark to you. To all of you. Nothing else. Nothing more."

The betrayal glistening in her eyes is like a dagger plunging through my heart. "Please, understand. I had to be sure. It's our survival. You understand that, right?"

She exhales and storms off. "I'm going to change. I'll meet you three in the living room. We'll have to go up together. You don't have clearance to leave the bunker."

As she leaves us in her wake, I draw a labored breath and push at the soreness in my chest. "We hurt her, brothers. I don't like that."

Link shrugs. "We had to be sure. You did nothing wrong, Flash. Come, if they speak the truth, we must get ready to go outside for a mission."

"And if it's a trick?"

"Then we might have our chance to escape."

~

Lark

I feel like a fool as I finish changing and pull on my boots. Why did Flash grabbing my hand affect me like it did? Why do I even care?

I know why.

In a community where everyone is against me and judging my actions, I felt a kinship to the three. I thought, if anyone would understand what it's like to need someone to trust them, it would be them.

But they don't trust me.

I finish buckling my boots and sheath my dagger against my thigh. Maybe the reason they all think I'm foolish is because I'm a fool.

With my chin up, I stride out to the common area. Flash hustles over to intercept me on my way to the elevator and I avoid his touch. "Don't. If you're ready, let's go. If you're not, then get ready."

"Lovely, please."

I meet the man's gaze and don't let any of my feelings leak through. "Don't call me that. I am a Biome General here to observe your traits and tendencies, not to become your friend. I blurred that line, but you set me straight. Now, we are expected up top. Either you're ready to join me or you're not."

Link steps in behind Flash and meets my gaze. "We are ready."

Turning on my heel, I access the elevator, key in my clearance code, and press my pass against the scanner. The elevator ascends silently and the four of us are equally quiet.

When the doors open, I stride out first. Lukas and Mac are standing with three other Alpha Squad soldiers near the exit. The soles of my boots thump out a steady rhythm as I cut the distance between us. "Gentlemen."

"Good, you're here." Lukas ends his conversation and leaves

the others to come address our group. "Welcome to the surface, soldiers. From what we've discovered in your files, it seems you three have never been outside the bunker."

"That is correct," Link says.

"I'm going out on a limb here, boys. Some of us are concerned about allowing you access to freedoms too soon, but after reading Lark's report last night, I'm hoping she's right and you simply need us to believe in you. You have quite a champion in her, you know."

"She has been kinder to us than we deserve," Flash says, sending me a pleading look.

I turn away and address Lukas. "What is our objective today, sir?"

"You all know Alpha Squad was attacked. Our team followed a vehicle believed to have fled this compound and we moved in to intercept and investigate. The countermeasures they experienced left us with one fatality and multiple serious injuries."

"My deepest condolences to your team, sir, and the family of the man you lost," I say, meaning every word.

"Thank you, Lark." He offers me a sad smile and then looks to the three. "What I need from you is both your knowledge of the biogenetics program you are part of and the men behind it. We don't know if it was Andras Brass who fled from here yesterday or Queen Laryssa's men or a private interest group or more soldiers who took over their own destinies. We need to figure that out."

"We have been in stasis for over a decade, sir," Link says. "We don't know any more than you."

"No, but we've been going through the specs we found and know you can interface with the systems and navigate the servers where the information we need might be held. Helping us track down these men is in both our best interests."

Link falls silent for a moment and Shift and Flash get that faraway look on their face.

Lukas's gaze narrows and I know he's questioning what is going on.

I think about keeping their secret but realize they have no loyalty to me, so I don't have to feel bad about being up front with my superiors. "Through Link's awakened enhancements, he has been able to create a shared neuro-link with his brothers. They're having a private conversation."

Lukas looks them over and grins. "That's incredible. I can only imagine how much that would help in battle. Comms are good but they only work for spoken word and there are many situations when we go completely dark and off comms. To be able to think conversations is amazing."

Link keeps his expression free of emotion. "It is a new ability. And yes, there is much we are still processing. Being able to speak privately to one another has been advantageous."

A shrill whistle from the door draws our attention to Mac, hanging inside the opening. "Are we doin' this or what?"

"Yep. On our way." Lukas raises his hand and gives him a wave. Then he glances at the three. "Stay close, listen well, and don't do anything stupid. If you step out of line, we'll take you down. I'd much rather work together but if you force our hand, we won't hesitate to haul your asses back here and pull the plug on this whole experiment."

Lukas might miss the flash of hostility in Link's gaze, but I don't. I recognize a rise to retaliation because I see it every morning and night when I look in the mirror. As quickly as it surfaces, it's gone.

I understand them not wanting to be threatened but is that all it was? I suppose we're about to find out.

CHAPTER NINETEEN

Mac

We bump across the rough terrain of the Dornte Fringe and unlike the first trip there, I don't stand on the running board and ride shotgun. I don't think my legs would hold me. I'm still as weak as a kitten and as wonky as a drunken sailor.

I promised Lukas I'd hang back, but there's no way I'm getting benched for this. Thankfully, he knows me well enough not to even try.

"You look like shit, boss." Brody's gaze is glued to the dicey terrain, but he casts me an annoyed glance. "With a magical healing and phoenix tears, you should be better. What aren't you telling us now?"

"Nothin' at all, lad. I'm as good or bad as I am and that's all I know."

"You're a stubborn ass who almost got himself killed and left us without a team leader. Despite the red-headed Highlander vibe you've got rocking, you're not Braveheart."

I chuckle. It's been a long time since he was pissed enough at me to start slinging Braveheart remarks. "Aye, ye got me dead to rights on that."

He grunts and says nothing more for the rest of the forty-minute trip.

As we park in behind the other vehicle, I pull the latch on the door and drop out of the truck. Despite feeling like I'm a splat of bird shit on a windshield, I straighten and tighten up.

No one wants to see their commander as a mortal human being. When going into battle, soldiers need to know they're being watched over by someone strong and unstoppable.

No matter how weak and stoppable he might feel.

"Mac. Welcome back!"

My squad closes in, and we get the knuckle bumps and shoulder slaps out of the way. When Dune and Tundra stride in, Alpha Squad gives them a royal reception and parts like the red sea.

Tundra meets my gaze and holds out his arm. "Blessed be, my friend. It's good to see you on your feet and back to battle again."

We clasp wrists and I take strength from our clenched hands. "It's good to be upright."

Dune greets me next. "You look a hell of a lot better than the last time I saw you."

I pull the male in from our clasped hands and hug him, slapping a strong hand on the back of his shoulder. "I owe ye my life, brother. Anythin' ye ever need, it's yers. I'm in yer debt."

"Nah, I don't want that," Dune says stepping back. "I do love fighting with you and Alpha Squad, though. I didn't want anything to ruin our fun."

I laugh. "Yer welcome to join us anytime, my friend. Consider yerself Alpha-D."

"Sweet," Dune grins and waggles his brows. "I have a call sign."

Tundra laughs and drags Dune over toward Lukas.

"And on that note," I say, grinning at my team. "Tell me what we've got, lads."

"Right this way, sir," Tazz says,

My team leads me through the charred remains of the old barn. The ground radiates heat and there are piles of rubble still steaming. The scent of bonfire is rife in the air and sets my cat on edge.

When we stop, I make a slow, runway turn to gain my bearings. The door we entered from was there... the truck there...

I find the spot where Dwa died on the blackened ground and wonder if the density of the black soil is truly worse there or if it's my imagination.

I take a knee and press my hand into the warm ground. "Safe home, soldier. I wish ye nothin' but peace and happiness."

"Amen, brother." Lukas hands me a rag to wipe the soot off my palm but it does little to help. "So, this is what we found."

He directs me over to where Josie is sitting on a camp stool. She's got a laptop perched on her knees and is frowning as she keys things in.

"Any luck, Josie?" Lukas asks.

"Not a lick. Obviously fae technology is different from what we have in our realm, but this is next level stuff. I'm not sure who developed their security encryption, but they deserve a bonus."

Lukas hitches his thumb over his shoulder and smiles. "That's why I brought them."

Josie glances over to the three and nods. "Give me the one with the enhancements in communication."

"That's Link," Lukas says, picking the guy out of the triad.

Josie sets her laptop down and gestures for him to join her by a metal panel in the dirt. "I read the specifications in your file. What I need you to do is access this biometric plate and convince the system you're allowed to gain access to the tunnels below."

"What makes you believe this system will recognize me?"

Josie grins. "Because I read your specs. Didn't I say that? I thought I said that."

I chuckle at her sarcasm. The woman is one of the smartest tech support soldiers I've ever worked with but she's just as wicked with her sass and her sidearm.

Link doesn't seem to appreciate her attitude, but then again, he doesn't seem to appreciate anyone around him other than his fellow freaks.

"You're looking much better." Lark moves to stand next to me to watch the two soldiers working on gaining us entry.

"Aye, weel, yer drugs knocked me flat on my ass fer the night. I suppose, given the choice, opting for a full night's sleep would've done the same. Although, we won't know because ye didn't give me a feckin' choice, did ye?"

I let her see the ire I carry about that, and the rumble of my cat's growl rolls at the base of my throat. "Lie to me again and I'll put ye on yer ass. As it is, we're done, the two of us. I'll not work with someone who breaks my trust."

"Don't be like that. You were in bad shape. I knew you needed more rest and you were suffering. I was trying to help you."

"Aye, well, that's not much consolation. What if I'd been in a dangerous position last night? What if somethin' happened? If yer boys there had shown their true colors and slit our throats in the night, I wouldn't have had a chance to defend either of us."

"If her boys had wanted to slit your throats in the night, you wouldn't have had a chance even if you were awake." I follow the hostility to the healer glaring down at me.

The moment our eyes lock, the buzzing in my skull subsides. Relief washes through me in a heady rush. As much as I can't stand being too close to the guy, the relief from the chaos in my head is almost orgasmic.

"I was speakin' to Lark, if ye please."

"You were speaking *about* us. I think that gives me the right to weigh in. How can you think I would hurt you or let anyone else hurt you? I told you. We are bound. You are my male."

I suck in a breath and glance around meeting the wide-eyed surprise of my men.

Fucking hell.

Gripping the male's arm, I tug him beyond the charred remains and around the side of the vehicles. Heading down the line of trucks, I get as much distance from the barn as I can. "Ye can't be sayin' shit like that in front of my men. Do ye get that? I'm their leader. None of them likes the idea of genetic soldiers. It's an afront to everything we are."

He leans forward and presses into my personal space. "I had no say in my creation. How can you hold that against me?"

"I don't. Obviously yer not to blame fer bein' created, but that doesn't mean I want ye tellin' people we're bonded."

"But we *are*. Lukas made it very clear that we must speak the truth or risk being put back in stasis. I don't want that. The truth is your cat bit me and something happened between us. It was involuntary and unexpected, I understand that, but the truth is everything within me craves you and I know you feel it."

"I don't. Yer reachin' fer somethin' that isn't there, lad. I'm sorry—"

My back hits the side window of the truck as the healer pins me against the vehicle. His lips are hard on mine, his hips pressing forward. The world spins as I'm lost to sensation, utterly overpowered and at the mercy of his passion.

And damn... the guy has passion to spare.

He may not have finesse but what he lacks in moves, he more than makes up for in hunger.

My cat roars inside my head and for a moment, I lose control on my beast. Gripping the guy by the sides of his jaw, I devour him. My tongue breaks the seal of his mouth and finds his. Lashing and swiping, our tongues parry.

He groans and grinds hard on me, the friction of fabric rubbing against my stiff cock too much.

It's so wrong...

But I can't stop...

But I have to...

I break from the kiss and try to suck enough oxygen into my lungs to clear my head. "My men... I can't do this. Not here."

I've barely gotten the words out when Shift's hold on my hips tightens and then we're in the air.

What the fuck? Wings.

He's sprouted motherfucking wings.

That reality hasn't even hit before we land at the edge of the forested area two-hundred yards from the scene of the fire.

"Here then," Shift says, pulling the shreds of his shirt off his shoulders, his wings now completely retracted. "You want privacy? I give it to you. You want other things too. Take them and it will remain between us."

"This is insane," I growl, running a hand through my hair. "We're not bonded."

Rough fingers are working at my belt, and I curse, fumbling to stop him. He's quick and strong. And if I'm being honest, I'm not sure what I want.

The sliding hiss of metallic teeth opens my zipper and a rush of air hits my heated flesh. My pants are yanked down to the top of my boots, and he pushes me back against a tree.

Dammit. I haven't had a quick fuck against a tree since I was a teenager. This is crazy.

Another zipper is dropped and then he's standing there naked in front of me. "Fuck, yer gorgeous."

Of course, he is.

He's liquid fire... a chiseled statue designed for perfection... designed for optimal performance.

I'm about to come to my senses when he drops down in front of me and sucks my cock into his mouth. His lips split over my crown and my breath is torn from my throat in a rush.

As he grips my sac, my vision blinks in and out of focus. I actually see stars spinning in my mind.

The sensation hits like nothing I've ever experienced, and I grip the back of his head, thankful to have something to hold onto as I lock my knees to keep from assplanting in the forest scrub.

As the bombardment settles into a hot and heady need, I glance down and watch his cheeks hollow as he sucks me off. "Fuckin' hell, that feels good."

There's nothing romantic about this.

It's full-on need. I close my eyes as he takes my length to the back of his throat, and I give the guy points—he knows how to suck cock.

My cat roars and the predator in me takes hold.

I grip the soft, golden hair clipped short to his skull and pump my hips. "I won't last long like this. It's too good."

Pressure is building at the core of my body, cum tingling hot, deep in my balls. It's the most messed up foreplay ever and I'm ashamed I'm getting off on it—but I am.

I *soooo* am.

Maybe it's the magic of his healing or me nearly dying and needing to live large or who the fuck knows... maybe we *are* bound by some fae universe bizarre twist of fate.

All I know is that I need inside him more than I've ever needed anything in my life.

My breath is coming rough and fast when I pull him off my cock and meet his gaze. He glances down to where my hand slides to stroke and tug, keeping myself good and hard. "Yer sure about this?"

"I'm sure. Take from me your body's desire. Punish me as

long as you need to excise your hungers. When we're done, we'll return to that barn, and it will never have happened."

He's serious. He's breathing heavy, his body ripped and flexing with anticipation.

I must be out of my mind. "Switch places and brace yourself against the tree."

He submits without hesitation. Facing the solid column of the tree, he presses his palms flat and gives me a glorious view of his ass. All that golden skin clinging over the musculature of a warrior is enough to make me come on the spot.

Damn him. He's right. I need this.

Still, I'm not a barbarian. Stepping in tight to his ass, I reach around his hips and grip his shaft. "Have ye been fucked like this before?"

"No," he grunts, pushing into my palm.

"Aye, weel, it can be painful at first. Give me yer release and it'll help." I stroke my free hand over the smooth, muscled plain of his back and wonder where those wings went.

Magic. It boggles the mind.

With a punishing stroke, I toss him hard and fast. This is a stolen moment to take the edge off and we both know it. When his breathing hitches, I reach around to catch the warm cum in my palm.

His body shudders as his release ends and I ease back to put things to good use.

Gripping my shaft, I sweep the engorged tip through the moisture in my palm and then put the rest where I need it. "Last chance to walk away."

"You are my male. Do it. Claim me."

My cat surges within me and I work my thumb into his ass, readying the muscles. I don't know about claiming him, but I'm certainly going to fuck him.

With one hand gripping the bone of his hip, I thrust forward and breach the constriction.

The pleasure is immediate.

Shift

The moment my male claims his desire, I'm washed with the most exquisite burn of pleasure. He warned me it might be painful, but if this is pain, I want to be tortured by him for eternity.

The invasion is incredible and when he's buried to the root of his pelvis, it feels like his cock might push through my abdomen.

"Can ye take more?" he growls behind me.

I drop my head between my elbows and hiss. "I can take anything you give, soldier."

"Aye, then brace yourself."

Closing my eyes, I do as commanded and try to remember to breathe. The slapping flesh of our union fills my ears and I access my data record to save this moment forever.

With each forward thrust, his breathing grows rougher. My breath escapes in short bursts as well, my erection returning hard and fast as he grows more frenzied.

Bark scrapes my palms raw as I brace my position so he can fully impale me to the depths.

This is even better than I imagined.

I watched the replayed images of Flash joining with Lark yesterday and felt his pleasure through our neuro-channel. It was impossible for Link not to find his release, caught in the wave of passion as he was.

But this is different. There is a sensual sting and a power of aggression with my male that wasn't part of Flash's experience with Lark.

This isn't just pleasure.

This is raw and rough and everything I hoped joining with a warrior would be.

We need this. He may be angry and resent our bonding, but what his body and his beast crave can only truly be satiated by me.

Too soon he thrusts hard and locks his hips behind me. Throaty sounds fill the air as his fingers dig into the flesh of my hips. He shudders, driving into me with each warm surge of his seed.

The moment his release mixes with my system, more of my genetic abilities unlock. It's a tingle at first and then I'm washed with the most erotic pleasure as my senses overload.

I knew it. I knew we were bound.

A cry of orgasm tears from my throat, my muscles clenching and squeezing his sated erection. He reaches around my hip as before and assists my release, stroking me as my pleasure crests and ebbs to calm.

Panting for breath, Connor Mac collapses over my back, his heart hammering against my spine. After a moment, he lifts his weight and eases out of me.

I miss his presence immediately.

"Here, uh... ye might want this."

I straighten and accept the soft cloth he offers. Once I've cleaned myself, I focus on dressing.

He does the same.

I'm not sure what to say or do in this moment, so I leave it for him to determine. He picks up the remnants of my shirt and utters a soft curse. "Weel, they're gonna notice ye don't have a shirt, so we'll have to deal with that."

He straightens, glancing around the forest and then nods to himself. "There'll be a duffle of spare gear in the back of one of our trucks. Exit the trees over there and fly back to the vehicles. I'll walk over from the opposite direction and join the group after."

I dip my chin. "Thank you."

He draws a deep breath and frowns. "I'm not sure what the hell that was, but yer right about one thing... I needed it more than I can put into words."

"You feel better? Your insects, the buzzing, your hunger? Are you at peace?"

He finishes securing the weapons sheath around the thigh of his fatigues. "Aye, much better."

I nod. "If you ever want me again, I am willing."

He rubs a rough hand over his mouth. "That's not likely. I think I got ye out of my system. Let's leave it at that, shall we?"

When he stomps off the way he indicated, I release my wings and fly in the opposite direction and round the vehicles to claim a new shirt. It's a black warrior shirt like Connor Mac's and as I pull it down my ribs and smooth it over my stomach, I feel a crazy sense of pride. I'm wearing the uniform of my male.

And whether he's ready to admit it or not... he claimed me.

CHAPTER TWENTY

Lark

I watch Link and Flash over the next half hour, focused on their intentions. If I was wrong to trust them and encouraged Honor and her mates to give them a chance too early, anything they do while they're out here today is on me.

It bugs the hell out of me that I haven't got eyes on Shift, but by the way Mac dragged him out of here, I'm not surprised they haven't returned.

Something undeniable is happening with the three. I gave into it and I'm still not sure if I was played or not.

They say I'm their mystical catalyst and they feel this crazy pull toward me too, but I can't be sure. Especially not after Flash showed his true colors and scanned me back at the bunker.

"I had to be sure. It's our survival. You understand that, right?"

Flashes words echoed his apology but was any of it real? The male's engineered enhancements are thought transference, data processing, and intel retrieval. He's a bioengineered emotional manipulator. A spy.

And spies lie. It's in the job description.

Lukas and Honor warned me not to be too trusting and I walked right into it.

"Lark? Are you okay?"

I meet the curious concern in Dune's gaze. "Fine. My head is just spinning with too much going on."

"I know that feeling. Been there, made one hell of a mess of things."

"I'll try not to follow your lead then."

"Probably a good idea." He follows my gaze to where Link is working with Josie on gaining access to the door. "Trouble?"

I shake my head. "Not really. Just reinforcing some boundaries in my mind so I don't end up being blindsided."

"Okay, now I am very concerned. Have they done something to make you question their motives?"

"No. Not at all."

"Then what's with the internal wall building?"

I glance at him and sigh. "You don't really want to hear this."

His mouth curves into an easy smile. "Sure, I do. You're our third, Lark. Three biomes. Three generals. Tundra and I both want to build on that. We want to be partners."

I meet his gaze and if I wasn't already doubting everyone's motives and intentions, I might believe him. "You and Tundra are mated to Honor and Lukas. The four of you are already partners in life and the protection of the crown. I'm the fifth wheel."

"Nah, not at all." He glances over to where Lukas is chatting with Brody and Tundra. "The four of us have the advantage of trust and time spent together to chat casually about security ideas, but when it comes down to it. The three of us—you, me, and Tundra—are the Biome Generals. We've got lands to heal and an army to rebuild. That's on the three of us."

That reminds me. Dune volunteered to oversee the training

of new recruits to start rebuilding our Amberloq forces. "How is the recruiting going? Have you got your trials figured out?"

He sets a hand on my shoulder and smiles. "It's *our* recruiting and *our* trials. Don't exclude yourself from the process."

I laugh. "Wow. You managed to say that and sound sincere."

"I *am* sincere, Lark. We're all rebuilding here. All of Dornte suffered in different ways and it's our job to set things right and safeguard our people going forward. It's a big job and there's certainly enough responsibility to go around."

I like the sound of that. "Thanks, Dune. I appreciate it."

He shrugs. "Hey, I'm just being honest. And besides, who do you think young warriors would rather impress, us or you? I'll give you the answer. It's you. Hands down you're the sexiest Biome General in Dornte history."

"Now you're bullshitting me."

"Nah, it's true. I've seen the way the three look at you and it's not all professional curiosity. They're genuinely in awe of you and that's a great way to build a bond with them and get them to trust you."

Building the bond isn't the problem, but trust... yeah, that's the tough part.

"Thanks for the pep talk, partner."

He winks, grabs the end of my hair and gives it a gentle tug. "We're here for you, Lark. Anytime you need us or want to take on more, we're here."

"Good to know."

When Dune steps away, I draw a deep breath. Maybe I can turn this around. If their only objection to me being part of the Amberloq force is that I don't have the physical conditioning and warrior skills they need, then I'll train and be the best slecking warrior they've ever seen.

～

Flash

I stand alone against what was once a corridor back to a stable of horses and observe the people around me. The soldiers under Lukas and Mac's command. Lark, smiling up at her fellow Amberloq counterpart. Link, helping the female technician, though it's taking him so long there is no way he's even trying.

For a very brief moment—less than forty-eight hours—I thought I might be free of the alienation of the life we were created for.

Lark believed in us.

Our enhancements were coming online.

I joined her in an intimate moment which, by her own description, was incredible. Now it's over and here we are again. Shift dragged out of the room by his male, Link playing his games, and me left feeling underappreciated and rejected.

By my brothers, the other soldiers, and Lark—*my* beautiful Lark.

If Shift can claim Mac as *his* male, then I claim Lark as *my* female. My brothers didn't feel the slap of betrayal and doubt that hit her when I read her intentions. They sought confirmation of information and I complied.

They were appeased—I was not.

"Hello, brother." Shift strides in to stand next to me. "Did I miss anything noteworthy?"

"Other than Link playing games so the humans don't know how easily we can search and control the systems they're trying to navigate, no."

"He knows best about tactical deceptions."

"Yes, but he knows a great deal less about the emotions and relationships of the people in this realm."

"Is Lady Lark still upset with you?"

I meet his gaze and try to ignore the happiness glistening in his eyes. "Angry, confused, betrayed, disappointed... yes, she's still upset with me."

He pats my arm, his grin still in place. "The situation will rectify itself. Trust me, there is no holding back what is meant to be."

"And I suppose you're speaking of the bond you feel to your male?"

His grin widens. "He acknowledged the pull we share, and he claimed me in the forest outside."

In all the years I've shared with my brothers, there have been times I was frustrated with them, hurt by them, and even disappointed in them, but never have I ever been so keenly angry at their lack of regard for me and my situation.

Clenching my hands into fists at my side, I breathe deeply and smile. "I am happy for you, brother."

Shift pats my shoulder and strikes off. "I'll go see how Link fares."

Left in the silence that follows his retreat, I turn on my heel and exit the charred structure.

I can't breathe.

The air is cleaner the farther I stride from the ruins of the barn, and I find a large boulder to sit on. Closing my eyes, I tip my head back and let the strength of the day's sunlight warm my skin.

Alone with my thoughts, I realize how truly rare this moment is. Our neuro-channel is closed. We're out of the bunker. And no one is around to tell me what to do or think or feel.

It's strangely empowering.

Movement inside the line of trees in the distance sets off my senses. It's too far away for normal human or fae senses to detect, but when I open my eyes and cast a casual glance along the horizon before me, I focus my ocular scanners and find two humanoid forms observing us.

Since Shift and Mac have already had their fun in the trees, I assume the onlookers aren't from our group.

Lark stops beside my rock and searches my face. "You're not thinking of making a run for it, are you?"

Her words pierce my heart but what's worse is there's genuine suspicion in her gaze. I suppose I deserve that. I doubted her and now she doubts me.

"Where would I go? I have nothing. If I leave, I'll end up more alone than I am here."

I'm not sure what my comment means to her, but she seems to exhale some of her hostility. "Are you and your brothers not getting along?"

"What's to get along? They decide what's to be done and I fall in line. What does it matter if I disagree or get hurt in the process? I'm just Flash."

"You're more than *just* Flash," she says, frowning at me. "Don't let anyone make you feel less important or less impressive than they are. You're a good male, a smart soldier, and a good brother."

And an idiot for hurting you.

I shrug, my attention still split between my conversation with Lark and the two people spying at us from the trees.

When I say nothing, Lark waves her fingers in a gesture to move over so she can join me on the rock. Seated beside me, she bumps my shoulder with hers. "How's your face?"

I probe my jaw where she hit me and work the sore muscles. "It was a solid strike. The tenderness will ease in a day or two. The regret will plague me much longer."

She stares absently out at the horizon. "I understand you felt you had to verify Lukas's intentions in order to safeguard your brothers, but by reading me like that, you broke the trust we were building."

"I hurt your feelings. You feel I betrayed you."

"You did. I told you my thoughts were private and I would be honest with you. You chose to scan me instead of believing me."

I want to point out that Link needed the verification, not me, but what would that change?

"I apologize. It hurts me that I hurt you, but I don't know that there was any other option. Being told we were to leave the bunker was a shock and well beyond our range of experiences. Link was unsettled. I had to—"

The click of a weapon engaging sounds in the distance, and I launch, tackling Lark and rolling with her in my arms. Flat to the ground, I hold her behind shelter as the projectile hits and bits of rock explode into the air. "Two observers in the trees due south."

Lark taps her earpiece. "Alpha Squad, we're taking fire. I've got two hostiles in the trees due south of the parked vehicles."

"I got two more north of the barn," Mac whispers back across the comm channel.

"Flash and I are moving out to pursue," I add.

"We're right behind you, Lark. Sending you back up, Mac." When Lukas stops talking, Lark looks to me.

I help her up and we take cover behind the vehicles. When she looks up at me, every protective instinct I possess fires to life.

"Okay, soldier, how do you want to play this?"

Mac

I spotted them when I was making my roundabout trip back to the barn after my indiscretion with Shift. With my mind scrambled between the sex and the fact that everything going wrong inside me had suddenly improved, I almost missed the assholes creeping through the trees.

Almost.

Whatever happened a moment ago with the other group firing on Lark and Flash has fired up these two as well. Even with me treading lightly and moving with all the stealth of my feline side, they've caught my scent or sensed me somehow.

With no way to get any closer in this form, I strip off my clothes, and set my Sith side free.

I hate the transition, but I respect that my cat can do things I can't. And when I'm alone in a forest with two unknown opponents, with more in the wings, I'll take the discomfort of transition if it means I have an advantage.

As transitions go, this one goes better than most. Maybe it's the magic of Shift's healing energy still in my system or maybe my cat's still purring because we just had a wild forest fuck and he's strutting his stuff.

Whatever the reason. Shifting sucks less than usual, so I won't complain.

It's the work of a moment to race the couple of steps forward to find the perfect tree to take me to higher ground. The wide pads of my paws come down on the leaves and twigs as I gain speed, and with a running leap, I launch into the air, grab hold of an angled tree, and climb for a better vantage point.

When I'm camouflaged in the canopy, I fall still and watch the two men below. Soldiers, for sure. No rural hiker or game hunter would move the way they do or carry the weapons they have with them.

And they know I'm here.

The way they stick to their cover and remain on guard tells me they are very aware of not being alone out here, but they haven't figured out where or what I am. Not yet anyway.

With Lukas on the way, there's no sense in waiting. Distraction is the best cover I can give my men as they move in.

Dropping to the branch below, I take a run and launch through the air. My cat lets off a snarling *mrowl* and I catch one of the intruders unsuspecting while startling the hell out of the second.

He calls for backup but there's nothing to be done about that.

The one I've taken down squirms, fighting against my hold. Kevlar vests and long-range rifles are no defense against speed, strength, and dagger-sharp claws.

I go for the exposed flesh of his throat, tearing and twisting, and he falls without a fight.

A pair of wolves race in from the treeline and my cat lets off a rumble of excitement.

Reinforcements have arrived.

Things just got interesting.

Battling animal to animal really gets the blood pumping.

As the forest erupts in snarls and the crack of gunfire, I dig in and take on the wolves. They are stronger, but I'm quicker. The offensive force of two against one makes for an exciting battle.

The shouts of Alpha Squad sound off around me and the game is on.

I swipe at one of the hindquarters of a wolf and send him spinning into a tree trunk with a yelp. His battle partner snarls and turns on me, fangs borne. He's fast, but I'm smart. With two running strides, I leap at a tree, push off the wide, bark-covered trunk, and do a parkour rebound, soaring through the air paws out.

I wrap my hold around his head, all four of my limbs shredding the fur beneath my claws.

Blood sprays the forest floor as Shift races to my side. He

wears a good deal of the spray, but as it smears across the perfection of his chiseled face, he swipes his fingers through it, and it becomes a fearsome war paint.

Fuck, he's beautiful.

A crush of goblins invades the forest and two are upon us in the next moment. We get back to business.

Shift makes a spectacular spin and cracks one of our opponents across the jaw with his boot. Man, he's strong and damn flexible. That shouldn't amp me up as much as it does.

I try not to think too look too closely at that.

The wolf with the bum back leg is snarling head down and backing up to keep us away.

The only way he leaves this forest alive is by retreating and he knows it.

The second goblin barrels forward and takes a run at me, I snarl and leap up onto my back paws, pulling him to the forest floor and rabbit-kicking his belly.

I'm getting washed by the warmth of his blood when the gleam of a metal blade catches the light above my head.

Shift curses, snatching him off me and hurling him into the closest tree. The crunch of bones ends him as a threat. To prove that point, Shift kneels beside the fallen and grips his head.

The crack of bone reverberates in the air.

With a violent twist, the man convulses once and then falls to the ground, his head cocked at an unnatural angle. Shift might be designed to be a healer, but he's got killer in him too.

I get back to my feet, brush his thigh as I go past, and head toward the others.

I don't need to worry.

The battle is won, and Lukas is assessing the dead. "Is everyone good?"

I shift back and shake out my muscles. Without the thick coat of my pelt, being naked in the shade of the forest is chilly. Even with the heat of battle still warming my blood.

Lukas lifts his head and scans our team. "Brody and Tazz, you're with me. We'll check the south group. Mac, you're sure you're good?" His gaze moves from me to Shift, and I know what he's getting at.

"Aye, we're good."

He nods and the three of them rush off.

CHAPTER TWENTY-ONE

Lark

With the promise of battle upon us, Flash pulls me to my feet, and we take cover behind one of the massive trucks. "Okay, soldier, how do you want to play this?"

Flash reaches behind his back, pulls at the neck of his t-shirt, and tosses the thing on the rock. Flexing his shoulders, wings burst through his back, and he stretches them out. "Mac's men can attack on foot. I suggest we take to the air and come at them from behind."

My mind stalls. "I didn't know you had wings."

Flash shrugs. "There are a lot of things you don't know about me yet. I can only hope you give me the chance to prove I can be more than you or my brothers think."

Before I can answer he pushes off the ground and launches into the midday sky. There's so much hurt and sorrow in him it bleeds through the bond we share. I hate to feel him suffering but there's nothing I can do to help him with that now.

Pushing off the ground, I join him in the sky and the two of us make a wide, sweeping arc to come at our attackers from the other side.

Flash points to a break in the canopy of the trees and then drops to land. Flipping feet first, he folds his wings back and practically torpedoes through the lush foliage of the leafy cover. I follow, giving my wings a couple of extra pumps to ensure he doesn't get too far ahead of me.

The two of us drop like meteors and land on the ground behind the men who shot at us.

Flash flexes his shoulders again and his wings vanish, and I'm left staring, mouth agape. I'm aware that many species of fae can retract their wings using magic, but I never even suspected Flash of having them.

I'm not sure why. Giving super soldiers the opportunity to fly in the field makes them even better suited to take on any problem.

The two of us are rushed by an opposing force almost immediately after dropping into position. The men with guns turn their weapons on us and I bring my wings around as a shield.

Elbirfae wings are almost impenetrable.

It takes a few tries to direct the ricochet the way I want, but after a few of the incoming bullets start embedding around their heads, the two abandon their guns and come at us with blades and might.

Fine by me.

After the time spent with Flash and Link this morning working on my fighting skills, I feel more confident than I ever have. I'm not so arrogant or foolish to think I'm invincible, but two on two doesn't worry me.

Flash offers me an encouraging smile. "Remember... step back, assess, and make your efforts count."

"Got it." I'm feeling confident until another rush of opponents join the fight. "Flash?"

The male growls and shifts closer to me. "Mac's men are almost here. Stick close to me and focus on staying alive until they arrive."

With that, the sweet and vulnerable male I know is gone and the genetic soldier locks in place. Punching, spinning, kicking... Flash takes on more than his share of attackers. He's beating down the opposing force four to every one of mine.

A solid strike to my cheek has my head swinging and my vision fritzing out in black spots behind my eyes. My body twists behind the momentum and then a sharp pain in my side sucks the breath from my lungs.

I turn back, my attacker still holding the hilt of the knife buried in my side.

I grab the hilt to stabilize it and swing my wing around with all the fury boiling over in me. It connects with his face. The crunch of his nose and the spray of blood staining the leaves around us takes a bit of the edge off.

Flash turns, sees the blood running between my fingers, and rushes forward faster than any normal male could move. He grabs the hilt of the blade, yanks it free, and drags it across the throat of my attacker.

I cry out as the blood flows more freely and then he's scooping me into his arms and launching us out of the fight.

The wind pulls at my hair, and I glance down to the tops of the trees. "No. We have to go back."

"Mac's men are there to take over. You need healing. *You* are my priority."

As much as I hate the gallant warrior rushing in to rescue the female trope, he's not wrong. He's also adorable when he's being protective.

I rest my head at the crook of his neck. "I'll get them next time."

"Of course, you will. There is no shame in regrouping when

you are injured and outnumbered. What matters is that you come back swinging."

"You're right." I kiss the side of his neck. "And you were wrong too, earlier. You could never be 'just Flash'. Not to me."

He pulls me a little tighter against his chest as he shifts to land. "Thank you for saying so."

Mac

Shift watches Lukas, Tazz, and Brody go and tilts his head the way all three of them do when they're confused. "Should we follow? Do we need to battle more?"

"No. Lukas will let us know if we're needed."

"If there are enemy forces in these woods, shouldn't we remain together?"

I smile and strike off back the way I came. "He's giving us a moment to decompress from the fight and allowing me time to find my clothes and get dressed."

"He never said that. Do you share a neuro-link with him?"

I chuckle. "No. Nothin' like that. Lukas and I have been battlin' together long enough that he understands when I'm fresh from a battle, I like to walk off my beast's hold and take my time getting dressed and pullin' myself back to the man."

Shift looks surprised. "Is your Sith feline truly a beast living within you as a separate entity?"

I spot the angled tree where I took to the canopy and retrace my steps. "Not separate, no. It's more like there are two parts of me to make the whole. Most of the time, it's harmonious but there are moments when there's a battle of dominance and we struggle to take control over the other."

He seems to consider that while I shake out my clothes and

pull things back on. "When we were naked in the stasis lab, you were quick to cover your body. Just now, with Lukas and your men, you showed no such concern. Why?"

"Again, Lukas and I have been soldiering together a long time, the same with my men. While no one wants to see one another naked, it's an unavoidable truth that it'll happen, especially with species that shift and can't manifest clothing."

I slide my arms back into my shirt and leave it hanging open at the front while I sit to pull on my boots. "When I covered up and asked ye to do the same, it was fer the ladies in the room. Lark, Josie, and Princess Honor wouldn't be offended, but it's also not right to simply strut around naked in front of them."

"But Lark enjoys us naked," he says.

I blink and my cat lets off a long growl. "What's that now?"

His brow pinches. "Why do you growl at me? Have I done something wrong?"

"I can't say. Have ye?"

He shakes his head. "I don't think so."

The question is, would he know it if he had?

I stand and gather the two sides of my shirt annoyed at the thought of what's been going on with Lark and the three and yet realizing how hypocritical it is for me to have an opinion after I succumbed to getting sexual with Shift myself.

Still, my cat doesna like it one bit.

"What does this mean?" Shift steps in close and trails a gentle finger down my chest. The contact raises the hair on my arms and my cat stretches languidly.

I meet his gaze and—dammit—the warm, whiskey gold of his eyes is swirling with hunger again. "The artwork and the metal ring?"

He gestures to the Celtic tattoos that run from the sleeve on my right arm, over my shoulder, and then down my ribcage to my hip. Front and back on my right side, it's a bloody masterpiece.

"It's the story of a great Celtic warrior who led the members of his clan in a devastating war. It's about a hero of my people."

"It's beautiful."

"Aye, it is. Thanks, fer sayin' so."

"And the metal ring?"

I lift my finger to my left nipple and flick the hoop there. "That's fer me and sometimes my lovers to enjoy. It's a bit of a turn on fer some."

He swallows. "I enjoy it. I would like to learn more about how your lovers utilize it during shared intimate moments."

I clear my throat and finish with the buttons. "Aye, weel, as I said before, what happened between us isn't likely to happen again. Whatever was pullin' at us, we've excised it now."

He has the audacity to glance down at the fly of my fatigues and smile. "Are you certain about that, soldier? Are you going to lie to me and tell me you aren't hungry again and craving more?"

Well, shit.

And just like that, I'm tumbling down the rabbit hole once more.

～

Flash

I fly over to the forested area north of the burned barn and see Lukas and his men running below. They're headed to the south to aid the men we were fighting with. Shift isn't with them. Neither is Mac.

For a brief moment I worry something might have happened to them. If Mac is injured, Shift would remain behind to heal him.

Then again, if Mac was injured, his men wouldn't simply abandon their leader.

Another scenario of what might be occupying them comes to mind. Perhaps I'm bringing Lark into a private moment between my brother and his male.

Will he be angry with me?

I disregard my hesitation. Lark's injury is more important than a moment of embarrassment.

I drop to my feet and survey the forest, shielding Lark with my wings as she did for me earlier. There are a great many downed opponents abandoned among the trees.

Mac's forces are mighty indeed.

I sense my brother's presence close by and send him a mental greeting, giving him time to adjust to the idea of our arrival. *I'm sorry to interrupt you and your male but Lark has been stabbed by the enemy.*

No need to apologize. If I can aid her, I will.

He can. I know he can. She is not nearly as badly damaged as Mac had been and he survived.

"All will be well, lovely. Shift will fix you now." I follow my sense of where my brother is and smile. It's not only Shift I can sense.

Perhaps his male truly is part of our destiny.

Shift and Mac are moving fast toward us and when we meet up with them, both are looking concerned.

"Bring her over here, lad," Mac says, gesturing a path through the trees. "There's a patch of grass just outside the forest where ye can lay her out and she'll be comfortable while he works on her."

I appreciate his consideration.

"You said she was stabbed?" Shift asks.

I drop to my knees and rest her on the spongy ground. She does not cry out when I lay her down and I acknowledge her strength with a smile. "Yes. We were greatly outnumbered. She fought well but the injury couldn't be avoided."

I meet their gazes, challenging them to say anything to the contrary. It hurts her to be judged on her fighting skills. She has gathered her knowledge as life turned on her and has never had the chance for formal training. I won't allow her to be shamed for that.

Mac shakes his head and glances down at Lark. "Looks like I'm not the only one bein' claimed. Seems our boy Flash has got it bad fer ye."

I scowl. "If you're making a comment about Lark being mine, then yes, that's true. If Shift can claim you as his male then I claim Lark as my female and I challenge you to say I'm wrong."

Mac holds his hands in the air and chuckles. "Oh, I'm not touchin' that challenge, lad. I don't know what the hell is happenin' between us. It's somethin' heady and powerful, but I have no idea what."

Shift pulls Lark's shirt up to the fabric binding her breasts and then unzips her pants and I help him tug them a few inches down her torso. "Flash, take her hand and keep her focused on other things."

Lark lets off a throaty laugh. "I doubt that's going to happen."

"Oh, it'll happen, lovely." I clasp her hand in mine and start reliving the moments I've filed away in my data storage.

When Shift presses his hands against the gaping wound in her flesh, I revisit my treasured memories:

The first moment I saw her.

How my body burned for her during our first kiss.

The exquisiteness of being inside her as the pleasure of our joining reached its pinnacle.

Lark groans and her eyes roll back in her head as her body undulates on the mossy grass.

Mac chuckles and sits back on his heels. Running fingers through his russet red hair, he draws a deep breath. "Whatever yer doin', lad, it's keyin' her up good. She smells like feminine spice, sex, and the kind of promises no male can say no to."

"Who says I'd ever say no?" I lay on the ground next to Lark, slide my hand under the nape of her neck, and tilt her lips to mine. "That's it, my lovely. Forget the pain. Remember only the pleasure."

CHAPTER TWENTY-TWO

Link

While everyone runs around as the world erupts in violence, I use the distraction to interface with the program servers without the female soldier hovering. She and the two other soldiers who remain are keeping a steady watch on the forest surrounding the ruins of the building.

I use the opportunity to my advantage.

The systems are, indeed, programmed to interface with our algorithms, so it's the work of a moment to navigate the security protocols and gain access to the information I need.

Too soon, Lukas and his two Elbirfae mates return with the bulk of the soldiers. He speaks to the female soldier for a moment and then strides straight at me.

When he stops before me, he points to the access screen. "Time's up. Obviously, you don't have what it takes to get the job done. Back to the bunker you go."

"Excuse me?"

"Hey, don't take it personally. You were decommissioned for

a reason. It is what it is. If you're useless in the field, you've got no business being here."

I straighten. "You know nothing about my capabilities."

Lukas frowns. "I know you're intentionally fucking around. I know you accessed the system over twenty minutes ago and you're milking your time out here. I also know that your delay in reporting put this entire expedition in danger. It's bullshit. I'm pulling the plug. Consider this your last outing."

Perhaps I underestimated them.

I press my hand on the data pad, grab the handle and pull the trap door open. "Access to the escape tunnel, sir."

Lukas glares and lifts a finger to point in my face. "Don't fuck around with me, soldier. I don't give two shits if you're engineered to be a god, if I can't trust you, I'll put you down."

"You could try."

The smile that curves his lips is confident and promises violence if I misstep. "Oh, I'll do more than try, asshole."

"What's going on?" Lark arrives with my brothers and Mac. Her shirt is torn down the one side and there is a great deal of blood on her clothing.

And her hands.

And Shift's hands.

And Flash's hands.

I step back from the confrontation with Lukas and stride over to greet them. "I could ask you the same question. What happened?"

"I just told you," Lukas snaps, following me. "While you've been sitting here playing your little games and gaining intel you chose not to share, you left us exposed and nearly got your beloved catalyst killed."

I meet his gaze and show no reaction to his accusations. "I'm sure I don't know what you mean."

"And I'm sure you don't recall me warning you that to lie to me and prove yourself untrustworthy is a sure-fire way to get yourself stuffed back in those stasis cylinders."

"No," Flash shouts stepping forward. "Link has trouble trusting but that's not his doing. We've had nothing but rejection and abuse from anyone we've met up until now. You can't threaten us with stasis every time one of us makes a mistake."

"He's right," Lark says. "They've spent the past twelve years locked in their own minds, aware that they are alive, but not alive. Unable to move, to communicate, or to wake beyond the most basic cognitive functions. As we build trust there will be missteps on both sides. Threats have no place in this."

"Neither do games," Lukas says.

I dip my chin. "I meant only to gather enough information to protect my brothers, should you try to decommission us once more. And let me be clear, we may have obeyed in the past, believing our makers had our interests in mind, but we will not make that mistake again. We will not be going back into stasis no matter the intentions of anyone in this realm. We would rather be destroyed."

"I can get behind that," Lukas fumes.

"It won't come to that." Lark's tone is harsh, as she stands her ground. "I will work with them. We'll build the trust needed, and we'll eliminate the need for threats."

"I'm with Lark on this," Dune says. "We know how Honor suffered being locked in her own form of stasis. There's no way she'll sign off on doing that to another person. Warriors don't always act according to the expectations of their superiors. That doesn't mean they can't be brought into the fold and make great team players with a little perseverance."

Tundra scoffs, washing him with a private look. "A *little* perseverance? I can't believe you can even say that with a straight face."

"Objection noted." Lukas smiles over at the two of them and his anger drains away. "If we can whip Dune into shape without strangling him, we can do the same for you three. That's if you start playing it straight with us. Don't fuck with us and don't try to put one over on us. We're smarter than you think."

I doubt that but decide to make a concession to appease him. "Very well, do you wish to follow the path of the underground tunnel, or shall I tell you what I learned about Valorous' soldier program?"

Lukas points to the open door into the floor. "First things first. These assholes killed one of ours and likely sent those teams to pick us off just now. We follow the breadcrumbs until things dry up. If you have intel about them, tell us on the fly. Everything else can wait until we get back to the bunker later."

With that, I step aside and let the first of his soldiers descend the metal rails into the underground.

Mac

It's fascinating to watch how Lark defends the three. Two days ago, she and I spoke of the abomination of scientifically designed soldiers. It seems we've both been forced to eat a whopping dose of crow.

Not that I like the idea any better—I don't.

It's just now they're real. Good or bad. Created or born. They are people. And whether we like it or not, they are in our lives.

As much as I'm fighting the attraction pulling me into their wake, I've seen fated couplings before and I wonder about the futility of trying.

Dwa died for this mess. He gave his life for a mission to secure the super soldiers and bring those involved in to learn what's been done.

I won't disrespect his sacrifice by trivializing it.

I also won't let the fuckers get away with it.

Once Lukas and Martin drop below the floor of the barn, I follow. The hollow *ting, ting, ting* of my boots on the metal rungs counts down my entry into the dark passage.

"It smells like a skunk's asshole down here," Brody says, wrinkling his nose.

My olfactory glands reel at the musky offense and I focus on taking shallow breaths. It doesn't stop the burning in my sinuses, but it helps calm the urge to vomit. "Imagine how it smells to a shifter."

Lukas cracks a light stick and the tunnel illuminates in a slime green glow. I pull a stick out of my vest and do the same.

Shift is at my side as I lift the thing to get a better view. He grimaces and looks away, closing his eyes.

"Have ye got night vision?"

"We have."

"I'm sorry. I didn't mean to blind ye."

He shakes his head and opens his eyes a crack. When that seems to go okay, he opens them the rest of the way and straightens. "No need to apologize. I've adjusted my ocular sensitivity. I should've anticipated the use of your group needing something bright. It's my fault."

"No, it's not," Lark says, frowning over at us. "These experiences are new to you. You weren't fully prepared, but you corrected the issue and will know for next time."

She doesn't hide her challenge as she stares me down. Uh-huh, the lass has grown quite protective of her charges.

Lukas raises a brow but doesn't comment.

Looks like he's got more than just me to worry about in regards to bonding with an unknown entity.

"Good luck, folks," Josie says from up top. "I've got your backs."

～

Lark

By the time we get to the end of the tunnel, we're tired and frustrated. It led us nowhere and taught us nothing. It was a simple back door escape to the other side of the trees where they probably had a secondary vehicle stored to offer them a means to escape.

I'm relieved to be back to the bunker. There's nothing I want more than to peel off the blood-encrusted clothing I've been wearing all afternoon. I've had enough of this day. "I'm taking first shower. Enter at your own risk."

Without stopping for any rebuttals, I storm back to my room, grab a clean outfit and my toiletries kit, and then head into the communal bathroom.

The day has been a disaster from start to finish.

Having the boys scan me for my intentions, finding out they're still playing their own game, getting my ass kicked in battle and ending up with a dagger buried in my side. So, why did I take on Lukas to save their asses, and risk my position when I don't know if they even deserve it?

I may have tightened my own noose on that one.

Time will tell.

Why am I putting my neck on the line for them? I've known them two days and yet I'm invested in their well-being. As crazy as it sounds, me being bound to them as a catalyst of some sort is the only answer that makes any sense.

And still, it makes no sense at all.

I examine the tatters of my top and throw it in the trash. Sometimes damage done is too much to fix. Sometimes the only option is to scrap it and move on.

The idea of scrapping my faith in the three nearly hollows me out. There's no denying it, something has bound us together and—for better or worse—Mac is part of this slecking mess too.

So, the three has become the five.

I open the faucets and stick my hand forward to monitor the spray until the temperature adjusts and I can step in. The shower area is an open space with four showerheads along the water wall behind the sinks. The walls and floor are tiled and there's a shallow ledge at chest height where I place my body wash and shampoo.

Behind me, a tiled bench sits out of range of the moisture and that's where I set my towel and clothes.

Settling in under the heat of the spray, I close my eyes and let the water wash the day away.

I feel like shit.

Not because of the stabbing—Shift took care of that well enough—but because, despite what people might think, I hate conflict.

Smoothing my hands over my head, I slick my hair against my scalp and exhale.

Flash was right. He hurt my feelings.

But what hurt more was that I let him inside my defenses so easily. If I hadn't, he wouldn't have been able to hurt me. There's nothing I can do about that now... The guy is seriously under my skin.

"May I join you?"

I startle at the sound of Flash's question and meet his gaze. There's so much emotion swirling in his eyes I have to look away to avoid falling into the abyss. "It's a big place."

He nods, gives me his back, and starts to undress.

Spending two years living in close quarters with more than a hundred people, I've showered with men before and thought nothing of it. And if it was any other man, it wouldn't faze me... but it's not.

It's Flash.

Turning on the faucet next to mine, he steps into the stream before it even has a chance to warm up. He makes a face at the showerhead, and I reach over to help him get sorted.

Once his temperature is set, I step back and focus on my own shower.

"Thank you, Lark. For all you do for me. I want you to know how much it means."

I draw my wings around to my front and run my fingers over the feathers, working any blood or filth out of them under the flow of water. And yes, maybe wrapping my wings around me offers a bit of a shield from my vulnerability, but I try not to think too much about that. "I understand why you did what you did, but you hurt me today."

He stops rinsing and turns to face me. "I know. And I regret it more than I can express."

I send him a warning look. "Don't do it again."

When he fists his hand over his chest, it feels like an oath. "I've seen inside you. I know your heart and I trust you. I won't allow my brothers to sway me again. I swear it."

I draw a deep breath and then turn my back to him, reaching for my body wash. "Then we'll put it behind us. I meant what I said to Lukas earlier. With everything that's happening there are bound to be missteps, but to build trust we have to work to overcome them."

Squeezing out a little glob of soap, I suds it up between my palms and focus on washing away the blood coated to my skin.

I jump when Flash leans in beside me and reaches for my shampoo. "Do you mind?"

"Help yourself."

My body is awakening to all kinds of erotic questions but I'm not about to take on more than I can handle. Maybe he's here for me or maybe he simply wants to wash off his day and apologize.

No expectations.

I finish laving my side and arms and watch the pink swirls of blood disappearing down the drain.

"Lenai blossoms, didn't you say?"

"That's right."

Stepping behind me he reaches up and starts lathering my shampoo into my hair. Strong fingers work up a lather, massaging reverent circles into my scalp. "You have lovely hair."

"Thank you." It should not feel this good to have a male's hands, working my hair into a lather.

It's decadent and sinful.

It's addictive.

"Now that we're out of stasis and able to regenerate, I think I will allow my hair to grow long like Connor Mac's. He doesn't look like a typical soldier, and I like that."

Damn, why haven't I had a lover wash my hair before? There should be a handbook of what not to miss when spending time with someone.

This should be on the top of the list.

"Do you prefer males with long hair or short?"

"I've never really thought about it... I suppose it depends on the male and what suits him."

"Then I leave it to you to tell me when to stop letting it grow." He reaches around me and removes the nozzle to guide the hand sprayer.

Tipping my head back, I close my eyes and drink in the relaxation of having him take care of things for me. "That feels amazing."

He finishes rinsing it out, gives the back of my wings a rinse, and then my ass and side. When that's taken care of, he replaces the showerhead and kisses my bare shoulder. "I will earn back your trust and protect it like the treasure it is. You are my female, and I will ensure I am worthy to be your male."

Grabbing his dirty clothes, he leaves the shower area, water still dripping off every angled plane and muscled curve of his very fine body.

I draw a deep breath of humid air and then exhale. *This has officially been my favorite shower ever.*

CHAPTER TWENTY-THREE

Mac

I'm in the bedroom at the end of the hall where I crashed last night when Flash comes strutting out of the bathroom buck ass naked and dripping wet. When Lark announced she was going in for first shower, I took that to be her wanting a moment to herself. Either I misunderstood or Flash did.

He wasn't in there long enough for much of anything to happen, but—

"Connor Mac? May I speak with you?"

The guy is giving me a full-frontal eyeful and I grab my towel from this morning and toss it to him. "Wrap that around yer hips, and then yer welcome to ask what ye like."

Flash does as I ask and frowns. "You told Shift that your need for us to cover our bodies was for the modesty of the females, yet my nakedness still seems to bother you. Why?"

I chuckle and rub a hand over my mouth, my head pounding with the absurdity of this conversation. What's with these boys and them asking awkward questions? "It doesn't bother me so much as cross lines of what's proper. People tend to cover their private bits around people they don't know well."

"So, nakedness is reserved for sexual intimacy?"

"Fer intimacy and moments when unexpected things happen."

"Like after you shift from your feline form."

"Aye, or someone being seriously injured and needin' medical attention, or things of that nature."

He falls silent as he seems to consider that.

As entertaining as it could be to have a stunningly built naked man in my room, I've had enough super soldier seduction for a lifetime. "Ye had somethin' ye wanted to ask me, lad?"

Flash looks up the hall and steps inside to close the door. "Link was able to access the server information at the explosion site. It would be in your best interest to question him about what he discovered."

As he's speaking to me, his voice is quiet, and his eyes are locked on mine. He's trying to tell me something without actually telling me.

"I understand the loyalty you feel fer yer brother and appreciate the nudge in the right direction."

He dips his chin. "I promised Lark I would never hurt her again. Link will not understand that promise or why it's important to me."

"Understood."

He holds my gaze and I think we understand one another. Opening my door, he steps out of my room, and collides with Lark coming out of the washroom.

The crashing of their bodies leaves them in a bit of a scramble and his towel drops to the floor.

When he doesn't automatically pick it up to cover himself, I bend down to do it for him.

That's when Shift comes into the back hall and scowls at the scene. "What is this?"

Lark holds up her hands. "I came out of the bathroom and crashed into Flash coming out of Mac's room. He grabbed me to steady me, and he seems to have lost his towel."

Shift raises a brow and scowls from flash to me and back again. "And what were you doing in the quarters of my male without your clothes on, Flash?"

"Och, don't be like that. He was askin' me about bein' a soldier and my views on a few things is all."

"And is there a reason why he did that naked?" Lark asks.

I chuckle and wave away her concern. "Only that he doesn't seem to comprehend when it *is* and *isn't* appropriate to wear clothes."

Lark laughs. "That sounds about right."

Link joins us in the back hall, and I take that opportunity to address Flash's concerns. "All right, how about after we've had a chance to clean up, we sit down over a meal and discuss what we learned today. Something is going on and I don't like the feel of it."

Lark rubs her towel around the wet ends of her hair. "I'll heat up the casserole Lukas brought and grill up some burgers to go with it."

"That would hit the spot, lass. Thanks." I nod to the three. "Take five minutes to clean up and meet in the kitchen. Lark and I both have reports to submit tonight and there are more questions than answers."

"No need to report," Lukas calls from the outer room. "We came to you and have intel to share. So yeah, everyone get dressed and get your asses out here. We've got shit to sort out."

Link

Shift and I follow Lark to the common area of our quarters, and are met by Lukas, Dune, and Tundra. The two Elbirfae are Lark's Amberloq counterparts, and they are mighty warriors indeed. It is no wonder she feels pressured to hone her skills as a warrior.

If they hold the standard to which she needs to rise, she has a great deal to improve upon.

Mac follows closely behind, pulling on a shirt. Flash follows soon after, fully clothed once more.

I admit Shift's draw to Mac and Flash's draw to Lark is unsettling. The three of us have always been a united force and I don't enjoy others being included in our concerns one bit.

Shift and Flash have both laid claim to others outside our group. Though we've never coveted anything or anyone, I'm not sure they will side with me if the need arises to protect our own interests.

Or, as we've learned countless times—*when*—the need arises.

Lark turns on the cooking appliances and Flash moves to the kitchen island to assist in meal preparation. He is utterly obsessed with her. Since when does he think for himself and not follow my lead?

I don't like this development one bit.

"Go ahead and start the briefing," Lark says. "I'm listening."

Lukas nods. "So, a few things we know for sure. The bodies you found inside the truck before it blew up have now been identified as two members of Andras Brass's team."

"But not Brass himself?"

"No. He's still unaccounted for."

Mac sits up straighter. "How did ye confirm that? Last I heard, ye had nothin' to compare the forensic results to."

"True, but Josie found their personnel files and the DNA samples they were required to submit before working with the program."

Mac sits back and rests his arm along the back bench where

he's sitting against the wall. "All right, so who killed them? The way I see it, there are only three options."

"Which are what?" Lark asks.

Mac lifts his hand and starts counting off his fingers. "They were killed by other members of the team, by an outside force trying to gain control of either their research or their creations, or there's a third generation of soldiers that got tired of being governed by their makers."

Lukas grins and gives him a nod. "Ding, ding, ding, we have a winner."

"How did ye find that out?"

Lukas grins and points to me. "Before I suggested that the three stay down here, I had Josie install a spyware program she developed to track anything that happened at any of the data points. Our friend Link has been a very naughty boy."

Impossible. He's guessing.

Only... when I assess his physical cues and analyze his voice patterns, there is a zero percent chance he's lying. "How...?"

Lukas narrows his gaze on me. "Every time you went snooping through the systems and opened doors for your own benefit, Josie's program recorded the access keys and left us back doors to use."

I swallow. "It seems I underestimated you."

"Overconfident assholes usually do."

I stiffen and he simply holds up his hand. "Don't bother. I get that you're new to the whole idea of trusting outside your circle, but it's getting old fast. Either you're aligned with the Thornebanes and we can work with you, or you're not and then you become a liability to the Crown of Dornte."

"We are not a liability," Flash says striding over to the table. "Princess Honor has our allegiance. We are her soldiers, the same as you."

"Only not the same," I correct.

Mac chuckles. "I think they named ye wrong, lad. Yer call sign should be Chip, not Link."

I don't follow his logic.

"Because you have a massive chip on your shoulder," Dune clarifies.

I glance to one shoulder and then the other. "I do not."

"We're getting off topic," Lark says, coming over with a platter of meat sandwiches. "No one here really knows the others well enough to cast stones, so let's try to work together, eat our cheeseburgers, and get to know one another without the bias of prejudice."

"Aye, that's likely a good idea." Mac reaches forward to select one of the sizzling sandwiches. "All right, Lukas. Tell us what Josie found."

Flash and Lark bring plates, cutlery, and a large dish of food to go with the sandwiches. As everyone helps themselves and heaps their plates, Lukas informs us of what they learned so far.

"A great deal has happened over the past twelve years while you boys have been in stasis. After the prototypes Alpha and Beta didn't meet Valorous' expectations, and the three of you were decommissioned as failed attempts, Andras Brass scrapped his preconceived notions of what super soldiers should be and began again."

"Och, to start again must've set him back years," Mac says. "Thank the stars fer that. If not, we might be lookin' at an *I Robot* scenario."

Tundra brings two small carriers of six bottles and sets them on the table to claim. Lukas grabs a bottle, twists the top off, and begins to drink.

Shift, Flash, and I observe and mimic the gesture.

As the liquid passes over my tongue, I scan my system to analyze the ingredients and determine it is a dark ale. As drinks go, it's not my favorite, but it is cold and flavorful, so I take another long drink.

"It took Brass almost five years of trial and error, but he finally came up with a working concept that he believed held promise," Lukas continues. "Instead of bioengineering a being from nothing, he and his team began gathering exceptionally well adapted members of the realm and converting them into soldiers."

"With what? Cybernetics? Reconditioning? Mental wipes?" Mac asks.

Lukas turns his bottle around on the table and shrugs. "Josie is still breaking down what was done and to whom, but it could be any or all of those."

I set my ale down and wipe my hand on my pants. "Forgive me if this sounds like me being an arrogant asshole, but how could adding cybernetic enhancements to a normal being make them a better soldier than the three of us? We have been engineered for strength, stealth, reflex, durability, intelligence, adaptability, and with our specialty enhancements now coming online, we have fae genetics to add to that."

Lukas nods. "For once, I agree with you, Link. From what we've learned, there were initial concerns about the hosts not being strong enough to overcome the physical alterations and learned responses from their first life. Valorous argued that depending on the life experiences, the soldiers could potentially be stronger."

"How so?" Lark wipes her mouth with a napkin before setting her cutlery across her empty plate.

Lukas addresses her directly. "Her theory was that if a young man was killed after watching his mother get strangled by an abusive stepfather, he would have a natural intolerance for abuse and a drive to protect the innocent."

Shift frowns. "Yes, but he would also be filled with rage and volatile emotions make for an unstable soldier."

"It could, but Brass and his people developed a serum to

counter that. As long as their soldiers continued to receive that serum, their emotions would remain stable."

"But if you're right," Lark says, frowning, "if it is the next gen soldiers who killed Brass and the other scientists, then there's no guarantee they'll still be taking the serum and if that's the case…"

Lukas nods. "Exactly. They'll become unstable."

Tense looks are exchanged around the table until Mac's cat lets off a threatening growl. "Weel, that's not good, is it?"

"Nope. Not at all."

"So, what do we do?" Lark asks.

It's Tundra, the ivory-winged warrior who leans forward to answer that. "We track them down and see what we're dealing with."

"That won't be enough," Shift says. "If what you're saying is true, it's more important to find out what their objective is and who's been influencing their programming."

Lukas sits back in his seat. "All right, I'm listening. How do we do that? From what Josie found so far, there's no trace of the profiles or the programming of the next gen models."

Shift turns his gaze to me. "Then Link will find you the information you need."

Ensuring my expression remains emotionless, I open the neuro-link to my brothers, and turn to Shift. *Are you honestly suggesting we help them? They are our jailors. The reason the other soldiers killed their keepers is because we are not meant to be kept.*

I disagree. Yes, right now, we are under their watchful eye but if we prove ourselves useful and our allegiance is no longer in question, we will gain our place among King Thornebane's quadrant.

When we prove ourselves useful, Flash pushes his thought at us. *I want a life beyond these concrete walls and would prefer Lark and Mac at our sides. If we oppose them, Lukas and his men will hunt us down as a threat. What kind of life will that be?*

Agreed. Shift says. *There is much to be gained by building a rela-*

tionship with the leadership of Dornte and fulfilling our purpose. We need to show them we can be valuable assets.

I draw a deep breath and exhale. "Very well. It seems we are in your service. And since my brothers are insistent that I trust you, there are a few things I'm certain you would like to know."

Lukas nods. "I'm listening."

"I was able to retrieve the security video of Brass exiting this facility with six soldiers and two other scientists."

"Six soldiers. Okay, that's not as bad as I worried."

"But during the time I was being 'naughty' as you called it, I found records of at least twenty other next generation soldiers who had completed their testing phases and were relocated to a secondary facility."

"Yer sayin' there are twenty-six more of ye?"

"Twenty-six more of them, not us."

Lukas exhales. "Well shit. You better show me what you found."

Lark

After the three finished their internal conversation about whether they are on team Thornebane or not, things seem to have turned a corner. Watching their faces, I could almost hear the argument play out in my head. Link being distrustful and superior while Shift and Flash explained to him that they want more than to be at the top of the food chain.

Flash wants to belong to something greater than himself. I believe Shift wants that too.

Thankfully, they got through to him.

At least for now, Link is working with us, instead of furthering his own interests. And with a bombshell like twenty-six super soldiers being unaccounted for, it's time for everyone to get on the same page.

Mac and Lukas escort Link to the interface console over by the elevator doors to begin work.

I rest a hand on Flash's wrist, trying to convey to him that I recognize he's doing his best. "All right, so while Link searches for the programming and directive information, we should brainstorm what else might be in play here."

"What do you mean?" he asks.

"Let's pretend you three weren't in stasis. The three of you are the next generation of super soldiers. You had a life, you've been reborn as a soldier, and then you learn a military squad is about to raid the bunker. What do you do?"

"We either fight or retreat depending on our plans and how much time we have."

She nods. "There is enough time. Someone tips you off, incoming forces are on the way and you have time to get out. Why do you run instead of fighting?"

Shift finishes his meal and wipes his fingers. "If their programming runs on the same logic as ours, we will retreat if we are not functioning at optimal levels and defeat is imminent, if our protocols dictate we mustn't engage, or if we have something or someone who mustn't fall into enemy hands."

Tundra meets my gaze and dips his chin. "Good. Now, you've escaped. What do you do?"

"We'd fly to safety," Shift says.

That's a good point. "Do you all fly?"

"We were designed to fight with the Amberloq army. The Elbirfae all fly. Yes, we all fly."

"But they drove," Dune says, reaching for another beer. "Is that because they were taking the scientists with them?"

Flash shakes his head. "More likely because the scientists took *them* somewhere. Then, once they were in that barn and the trap door was open, they saw their opportunity to escape."

"Or Brass ordered his soldiers to snap the necks of his assistants and took them for his own."

"For what purpose?" Tundra asks his mate. "What's Brass' motive?"

"There are only four reasons men do anything, money, power, love, or revenge."

I run my fingers through my hair. "Well, if he's now in control of Valorous' super soldier army, Brass has power and money at his fingertips."

"Maybe that's it," Tundra says. "Maybe after all the years down here developing the ultimate warriors, he began to think of them as his own."

"Especially after Laryssa overturned the Thornebane rule," Dune says. "When Valorous died he no longer had anyone overseeing his work. For the past two years he's been able to do what he wanted."

"Wrong," Lukas says, standing over Link at the interface console. "Link just opened the private logs of Andras Brass. Long before we killed Laryssa, she found out about this program through a journal Creed and Honor's father kept. She knew about the super soldiers and was pressuring Brass to add them to the force of her dragon guards."

Flash and Shift look blank on that one, so I help catch them up. "The Usurper Queen had two powerful dragon shifters as her enforcers—twin brothers—Rhylan and Vikarus. They were bound into servitude and when Creed and Honor reclaimed the quadrant Rhylan chose to stand with them and his twin chose Laryssa."

Lukas strides back to join us, frowning. "The important point of this story is that if Laryssa knew about the creation of bioengineered soldiers and made plans for them, you can be sure she bragged to her financial supporters."

Tundra curses and glances at his mate. "And if her financial supporters know..."

Dune holds up his hands. "Power and money, people. Brass couldn't let us take his toy soldiers because he knows what they're worth to the assholes still trying to undermine Thornebane rule."

"So, if we're right," I say, looking to Shift and Flash, "if you were being sold off to the enemy, what would your first objective be?"

"Take out the opposing force," the two of them say in unison.

Lukas curses. "We need to get back to the castle and fill Honor and Creed in on this. If they're coming after the Thornebane rule—"

An alarm sounds and the lights go out.

Plunged into total darkness, I freeze for a moment until the backup lighting kicks in over the door.

"What's that alarm for?" I ask.

Lukas hustles back over to the interface console as Link calls up the cameras in the bunker. Room by room, images start flashing up on the screen

"—There." Mac points to one of the pictures on the middle of the screen on the right-hand side. "Who are those assholes and how the feckin' hell did they get in here?"

Links fingers glide over the screen at an incredible rate. He catches the intruders as they glance up, scanning their faces, and pulling up soldier profiles one by one. "They are some of your missing soldiers."

"Shit, and they've come back why?"

Link casts a glance over his shoulder to all of us. "As my brothers said—to take out the opposing force."

Shit. We're under attack.

Thank you for reading Find the Fallen, book one of Lark's trilogy. I hope you enjoyed getting to know Mac a little better and meeting Flash, Shift, and Link.

While the story is fresh in your mind, and as a favor to me, please leave a review and tell other readers what you thought. A quick star rating and/or even one sentence can mean so much to readers deciding whether or not to try a book, series, or a new-to-them author.

Thank you.

And if you enjoyed it, continue with the Guardians of the Fae Realms with book 14 in the series.

Rise from Ruin.

ABOUT THE AUTHOR

Author Notes

Written on 28/09/2022

I hope you enjoyed Find the Fallen, book 13 of the Guardians of the Fae Realms series. It's great to be back to writing in this world again.

I took six months and focused on my Auburn Tempest pen name, writing my Urban Druid series and now I'm back to alternating hats.

I have two more trilogies planned for this series, Lark and then I think Remi the fairy bartender from the Gauntlet will show us what life is like in the Fringe.

We haven't met her on the page yet, but she's been playing out in my head. We'll see. There's really no telling which characters will speak to me from one book to the next.

Now that Lark's story is started, her story is unfolding in my mind, and I look forward to watching the five of them come together.

Don't forget to grab Rise from Ruin and follow the five as they leave the bunker and start to rebuild the Amberloq forces.

Wishing you a warm and wonderful autumn,

Hugs to all,

JL

The three have become the five.

As crazy as it sounds, I'm bound to three sexy, bioengineered super soldiers. In a moment of battle, with blood flying and passions heightened, Link, Shift, and Flash were not only freed from their stasis, their powers engaged. **I am their catalyst.**

I don't know what to think about that... Connor doesn't either.

With Shift imprinted on him and the three of them bound and bonded with me, it's a big mess. As the pull between the five of us grows stronger, Andras Brass and his army come at us, determined that the three never reach their full potential.

His first mistake was discounting them. His last mistake will be underestimating them.

Find Me

My Direct Sales Site: Shopify
My books
Web page – www.jlmadore.com
Email – jlmadorewrites@gmail.com
Newsletter – JL Series Updates

An action-packed fantasy romance series from International Bestselling author JL Madore and debut author Ruby Night!

They came for my twin and left me behind because women hold no power in the magi world.

They're about to find out how wrong they are...

Jesse Storme. Bartender. Rock-climber. And the girl left behind.

One minute, Wyatt and I are scaling our favorite rock peak and enjoying a moment of escape from our crappy lives. The next, **we're attacked, and my brother is gone.**

I think it's connected to the creepy recruiter dude from **Exemplar Hall.**

I find out it's so much worse than that...

Sucked into a **Hunger Games meets Harry Potter** event to rescue him, I don't know who I can trust. I'm a girl posing as a guy. I'm not supposed to be here. And I'm definitely not supposed to have the power I do.

Doesn't matter. I would suffer any pain to find and save Wyatt.

*We're more that twins—***We're Gemini Twins.**

ALSO BY JL MADORE

JL's Reverse Harem Titles

Guardians of the Fae Realms

Guardians of the Phoenix - Calli's Harem

Book 1 - Rise of the Phoenix

Book 2 - Wolf's Soul

Book 3 - Bear's Strength

Book 4 - Hawk's Heart

Book 5 - Jaguar's Passion

Darkness Calls - Keyla's harem

Book 6 - Dark Curse

Book 7 - Dark Soul

Book 8 - Dark Crown

Guardians of the Crown - Honor's Harem

Book 9 - Honor Restored

Book 10 - Honor Guards

Book 11 - Honor Bound

Book 12 - Honor Empowered

Rise of the Amberloq - Lark's Harem

Book 13 - Find the Fallen

Book 14 - Rise from Ruin

Book 15 - Trust and Triumph

Exemplar Hall

Exemplar Hall - Jesse's Harem

Book 1 – Captured by the Magi

Book 2 – Jesse and the Magi Vault

Book 3 – The Makings of a Magi Knight

Book 4 – Clash with the Magi Council

Book 5 – The Unstoppable Storme

Club Sanguine

Book 1 – Moonstone Maelstrom

Book 2 - Sunstone Sacrifice

JL's More Traditional M/F, M/M, or Menage

The Watchers of the Gray Series (Paranormal)

Book 1 – Watcher Untethered – Zander

Book 2 – Watcher Redeemed – Kyrian

Book 3 – Watcher Reborn – Danel

Book 4 – Watcher Divided – Phoenix

Book 5 – Watcher United – Seth

Book 6 – Watcher Compelled – Bo

Book 7 – Watcher Unfeigned – Brennus

Book 8 – Watcher Exposed – Taharqa

The Scourge Survivor Series (Fantasy)

Book 1 – Blaze Ignites

Book 2 – Ursa Unearthed

Book 3 – Torrent of Tears

Book 4 – Blind Spirit

Book 5 – Fate's Journey

Book 6 – Savage Love – epilogue novella

Aliens of Atlantis Series (Sci-Fi)

Book 1 – Taryn's Tiderider

Book 2 – Kai's Captive

Book 3 – Alyandra's Shadow

www.ingramcontent.com/pod-product-compliance
Lightning Source LLC
Chambersburg PA
CBHW020315260626
47156CB00004B/1236